MW00476152

THE NIGHT OF THE LAST KATÚN

...2012
Maya

Ac Tah
The man who talks

The Night of the Last Katún 2012 Maya

© **Copyright 2010**

All rights reserved under International and Pan-American Copyright
Convention

Cover design: Hayoka
English cover revision: Rick Williams

English Translation: Ananda
English Revisor: James Needham

Printed in Mexico

The Night of the Last Katún 2012 Maya

CONTENTS

The Night of the Last Katún 2012 Maya

Le maax ku yohela ku Tal ti u mas no'ochi chi'i' ibal ti to' on, le mako' obo maya'ab.

Leti ku yohelaje ba'ax tun kiuchu huaye, ku huila yete ku dzicbalik ton ca' achi ku sa'asta u bali u katún.
T' aan ¨Popol Vuh Maa yab

The one who knows comes from the Maa yab people.

He will know what is happening here, he shall see and explain. Then, the mysterious signs of the katún will be revealed.

Message from Popol Vuh de los Mayas

<u>Dedication</u>

I always wanted to write something for my daughter since she was born, to express how much I love her. I couldn't find the adequate language. When she was born she was like the star that I saw up in the sky before going to bed, since I was a little boy. The star that has guided my ancestors, generation after generation, and has become my guide and the corner stone of my life.

L'amat Itzel, thank you for choosing me as your father. All my life, all my efforts are oriented towards providing you with a peaceful, harmonious and loving world, so you can enjoy the awakening.

Introduction

I am Ac Tah, a direct descendant of the Maya; my ancestors have honored me, electing me as their messenger; the one to transmit to the world the knowledge and information scripted on the Mayan steles and glyphs. The great majority of interpretations of the Mayan heritage that we have read or seen in documentaries and films are mere speculations and, thus, are often mistaken or differ from the truth and messages that my ancestors really meant to leave us. Only the Mayan heart and nature are capable of interpreting this knowledge.

Regardless of race, creed, social class, gender or age, the contents of this book are of crucial importance for you because there is little time left and a lot to do if, indeed, you wish to participate and experience the awakening of consciousness where only unity, harmony and equilibrium shall exist.

The predecessor of action is thought, so whatever you wish for at this moment shall become your present in the near future. The present book is about the return of Kukulk'an Quetzalcoatl, the messages of light that were passed down to us by our ancestors, the calendar of the time count, and the last period of darkness for the Maya. It is addressed to all of those people who wish to work on behalf of the awakening of consciousness; also to those who perceive the changes in the planet and see their relationship with the people living in it. All of the revelations and anecdotes presented in the different chapters of this work were transmitted to me in various ways:

❖Visualizations: these are mental practices that open access to the spiritual realm.

❖Spiritual (inordinate) experiences that channel the higher energy frequencies into the three dimensional world we live in.

❖ Mayan meditation and *mantralization* procedures: these are guttural exercises that open access to a given brain vibration frequency.

❖Day-dreaming: it is when you dream while you are awake.

❖Daily personal inordinate experiences.

Some of you may have a rather skeptical stance before these matters, but as you become more familiar with the contents of the book, I am certain that you will see their truthfulness.

I THE NIGHT OF THE LAST KATUN

1. Sut' u suutukoob

(The moment has arrived)

Throughout this text, I will travel with you to different places to motivate you and acquaint you with the archeological sites of the three main cultures of Mexico: the Maya, *Aztlan* and *Mexica* cultures. Together they form the more encompassing *Maa yab* culture. I will also take you to different periods of time where I traveled myself, under the guidance of my ancestors. Our ancestors' heritage will stun you!

I must say that the term "Maya" has changed in time; the original, *Maa yab*, meant "the not many" or "the elected". But they were elected for what or why? The answer is simple: to transmit to you and remind you who you really are, where you are going and how you can use Mayan technology to elevate your body frequency to that of an awakened being.

It is also important to mention that the contents of this book have absolutely nothing to do with negative activity such as black magic or any other kind of harmful spiritual practices exceeding the precepts of love, peace and harmony. On the contrary, the information herein presented has been revealed to me by beings of higher frequencies. Their energy has helped me interpret the messages that our ancestors – the *Maa Yab* people- left for us to understand that the balance and synchronization with the Universe is not mere fantasy; that everything on the planet is related to us in a very personal way. As you will see in this book, the Maya legacy shall help us be prepared for the great changes to come. Such changes will bring about a totally different lifestyle for human beings, and most of all for the Mexican people, and for anyone living in Mexico.

So we now have the chance to take a quantum leap and to awaken our consciousness to live a spiritual life in a world of peace and harmony. This book is not just another manual for achieving "success in life", religious book, novel nor a science fiction book. It's a document aimed at warning you that we must act now, because the count down has begun.

We have little time!...So, when I count to 2012.... can I count on you?

2. Tin Tukultic

(The world of the "whys?")

You could say I was a normal child like any other; I went to grammar school, secondary school and high school. I never had excellent grades, nor was I ever on the honor roll; well, except one day in grammar school, when I got excellent grades for a beautiful painting that I turned in. But in general, I didn't like school and was only interested in subject matters like History, Geography and Spanish, and also in a little girl that used to sit next to me. I felt different from the other kids my age. In those years, it was not common for a little boy to ask so many questions, and I recall being a rather inquisitive little guy, except no one answered my questions. I was the kind of boy that thought a lot and analyzed everything. I questioned the things I was told to do and why I had to do them.

Since I didn't enjoy school, I decided to take up a job at an early age. I had many, many jobs but not one pleased me completely, although I did value what I learned from them. Early on I took to traveling to look for the answers to all of the questions that puzzled me.

I wondered about a lot of things: why I felt different from the other kids. Why I didn't enjoy any of the things that were taught in school, why if life was so simple and easy, most people complicated it with ego, control over others, fears, etc. Why was there so much poverty, evilness and social inequality in the world. Why must a human being struggle to get by in life; Why do we seek spirituality?...

I also questioned some aspects of daily life such as: why do we have to work if we are intelligent creatures? Why do we have to do things we don't like? Why do most people live in small houses where one step will take you from the living room to the dining room and from the dining room to the bathroom? Why can't people see that living in very confined spaces leads to family violence and dysfunctional family bonds? Why do people live in large cities if it stresses them so much? Why do people live in housing complexes and concrete cities if we are continuously striving to get away to the country or to the beach? Why as young people do we not care about our elders if we know well that we will reach that final stage ourselves, probably much sicker than them? Why do we assert that slavery does not exist if this is all we see around the world?

Everyone trying to enslave and control everybody else!

Why are lovers not happy?

Why do men have to go out to work and women must work in the house? Why is the world ruled by men, while women, who are better prepared to make decisions, are left behind? If women are responsible for children's upbringing, why don't they teach their children to respect them as they deserve, to have equality at home as well as at work? Why do men overpower women? Why are there values, moral standards and rules if everyone already knows inside what is right and wrong? Why do I ask myself all these questions? More philosophical questions also came to my mind like: why do they teach us that God is everywhere and then they tell us we must pray in a given place to reach Him? Why can't we see God? Why does God have secrets? Why do they tell us that God punishes and at the same time that He is love? Why doesn't God do anything to uplift humanity if we've been here more than 250, 000 years?

Why do I feel alien to planet Earth?, Am I from this planet? Why do most humans enjoy gazing up into the sky? Why do I feel so attracted to the archeological sites and to ancient things, but most of all to the Mayan life style? Why do I have the feeling that most of what historians and archeologists have written about the life of the Maya is not true? What does the number 13 (Oxlahum) mean to the Maya? Why are the prophecies and changes of 2012 ascribed to the Maya? Why are they talking about the return of Kukulk'an Quetzalcoatl? What's the relationship between the Spring equinox and modern life? Why is the Earth undergoing global warming?

If by any chance you've asked yourself any of these questions and you really want to know your mission in this world, I suggest you continue reading. This information is authentic, not far fetched ideas nor a bunch of "horse stuff" as my grandma used to say. It is indeed crucial for you.

3. A'hal

(The Awakening)

Imagine that we are today on the prophesied famous date of the Maya –December 22nd, 2012. On this day an interstellar beam will come from the center of the galaxy and will cross through our planet and in doing so will affect deeply every human being. As a consequence, consciousness will awaken and people shall become better. That same day, they say, evil will ceases to exist, we will all help each other and wish our neighbors well. There will be perfect understanding between men and women, we will respect each other. There will be no more illnesses, no more poverty nor broken families. There won't be any more robberies or pillage, and every single thing will exude harmony, happiness and abundance. Nature will be in perfect balance, and there won't be any more environmental pollution nor global warming. There won't be any more jails, egotism, fear or depression. In short, everything, absolutely everything will be in perfect synchrony and stability. And so, as we approach the fulfillment of the prophecy, all we have to do is to be tolerant and patient, and to sit down and wait, and wait until it happens....But, will it really be like this? Of course it won't!

What we do know for certain is that a planetary alignment will take place, and that a solar flare will reach out intensely from the center of the galaxy. But what is not going to happen is your becoming good and full of love and harmony in just a few seconds...Not unless you assume your responsibility and do something to contribute to the awakening of man's consciousness. And I mean you must start doing it right now. First, we need to create the neuron wiring, in our brain, capable of tapping this ancient knowledge. Otherwise, it would be like trying to communicate with someone who does not speak your language.

A lot of people are waiting for something extraordinary to happen, for

The Night of the Last Katún 2012 Maya

everything to change overnight without them having to do anything to make it happen.   At the end of the last century, many people thought they would face the end of the world as we entered the year 2000, but nothing of the sort has happened . We were all caught in expectation, yet nothing happened. Some even thought that God would be physically there to judge us, and that the good people would go to Heaven and the rest would be sent to Hell. We are still waiting for someone to appear with a magical staff in his hand to change the world, but that is never going to happen, because the shift towards a harmonious and well balanced humanity is not the responsibility of only one person, but of every human being on the planet.   You cannot assume your responsibility on December 22nd of the year 2012. You must assume it now, precisely today, as you are reading this book.

 As we approach the year 2012, people will be able to experience the spiritual world and perceive energies of different frequencies.   The Maya had a vision of the change of our geological Era and of a change in the human consciousness, by the year 2012.

I know that many people will feel reluctant to believe what they are going to read here, and will criticize the book's proposal for us to become synchronized with the Universe. Many people will disagree with my thinking, but I assure you that this is not just another theory and it is certainly not a personal opinion; it is the vision of spiritual beings who once walked in this world. It's the viewpoint of beings from other galaxies that want to help us because if we destroy our planet and ourselves, it will not only affect the synchronization process of humanity but of all the solar systems, known and unknown. And that is why it is crucial that we do something for ourselves and for the preservation of our descendents, and to do it now by reaching a higher vibration frequency.

4. In kaanb
(My learning)

On May 8th, 1967 I arrived on this planet at 5 pm., from the *Ac Caché* and the *Tah Baak* Mayan lineage, and from my mother's father and mother: *Tah Huchin* and the *Baak Bee*, respectively. I was born in the hallway, in my grandparent's house in Villa de Espita (*Xpit ha'*, which means "place where the water jumps"), in Eastern Yucatan, Mexico.

I was born under the family's ancestral traditions, my mother gave birth standing, wrapped in a hammock that could exert pressure on her body and hold her at the same time, while my father was helping her. This was the Mayan way. I was the last of my parents' eleven children, known in Maya as the *xtup* (the smallest or last one). The last names I bear are the true essence of my Being and mission; I always introduce myself as *AcTah* (talking man), very proud of expressing my indigenous lineage. My birth did not announce any historical event; there was no planetary alignment that day, no eclipse; the sky was not darkened. I was not born with some physical deformity [deformities at birth were a sign of godliness among the Maya.] I was not born different from other children. When I was born, important people did not attend my birth, but I was received by the important members of my family: my father, my mother and many others, all full of love.

Of my parents eleven children, three of us, Tere, Ruby and myself, lived in my grandparents house while the others moved to my parents' house in Merida, Yucatan, in order to go on with their education. Although I had the company of my two sisters, I was always a solitary and emotional child (I would cry over everything). However, what really stood out during my childhood was the education that I received from my grandparents. Here I refer to spiritual instruction not academic education.

My childhood was a very special one. I grew up in a very natural environment, where drinking water out of wells was still possible. There was no electricity, and that was exactly the kind of environment that

The Night of the Last Katún 2012 Maya

kept me in touch with nature and in close communication with my grandparents who brought me up with much patience, love and wisdom. They created a state of consciousness that made me respect our culture and honor our ancestors for their wisdom.

Memories of those sunsets without electricity come to mind: grandma would put an oil lamp over the table to give us light at dinner time. With a rustic fan she kept the wood fire going to heat up the handmade tortillas, and prepare that delicious steaming hot chocolate that my sisters and I loved. What we were most fond of was our grandfather joining us at the table and telling us stories about our Mayan ancestors, in the twilight. Such accounts have been passed down to us for generations, and I have never read them in any textbook. However, in the following pages, I will tell you how some of them became real.

I recall so many beautiful moments in my childhood including the occasions when my grandfather transmitted his wisdom to me. I remember his physical image well: a Mayan descendant heavily framed from working hard all of his life, he had an extraordinary wit, that I most admired and learned from. Many times we would sit on the door step at dusk and talk. He would show me the constellations and explain to me about the planets and the movement of the stars. He'd make my sisters and me wake up at 4 or 5 in the morning; when he would open the *wicket* –as we used to call those little windows on the doors- and he sang to us *cock-a-doodle-doodle-doo, no lazy ones are due!*. And with that innocent expression of his, he exclaimed, "Look how beautiful that star is; she came closer today to greet you good morning!"

The hammock where we slept was right in front of that *wicket* so all it took was to open our eyes to see the most beautiful sight you can imagine: a gigantic star that looked so near, you felt you could touch it. It was the morning planet Venus, that was about to disappear with the dawn. This seemed to be the stars brightest moment between the dark of night and the suns first rays that streaked the sky. I am sure that my sisters Ruby and Tere recall those moments with the same joy I do.

My grandfather taught us to appreciate nature, preserving in us a sense of balance, but most of all to be open and receptive. I remember going to the back patio with my grandfather, in the middle of the night, to communicate with beings whose very special trait was that they shone in the dark. I now understand they came from different planes. Because I was so young I never really analyzed what we were doing; I just did it and it seemed the most normal thing in the world. But my grandfather knew exactly what that was all about. He always encouraged me to be confident, and he emphasized that the world is not just what we can see, that there are a lot more things to discover. He told me that what I was learning then would be of use to me in the future. So all I did was listen.

Thanks to him, I learned to listen to people, and to interpret the vibrations and frequencies of alternate dimensions. My grandfather showed me how to connect myself to the Universe. I learned that everything was related to everything else (*In la' ak a la' akesch*). My whole life was built on the platform of love and mutual understanding. I was very motivated and curious to discover new things. I think that my grandfather knew who I was and why I had been born to his lineage. He knew I was a spiritual being that had been born with a mission, and that's why he gave me a special education.

Upon graduating grammar school, my childhood came to an end and I was sent to Merida, to live with my parents. Here I was to learn new things and complete my formal education. Among the new things I learned, was self sufficiency, taking risks, non attachment and emotional control. I spent my adolescence in silence as I was a very quiet boy; a stone would have talked more than me. People said I was shy but I thought of myself as someone who observed and spent time structuring his thinking. Just to give you an idea, I don't even remember any particular details of my education, but I do remember the friends I had at that time, some of whom I've met in my adult life. Although we don´t agree on many issues, I hope that if they ever read this book, we'll be able to sit together and discuss higher knowledge.

During this time in Merida, I learned a variety of disciplines like karate and athletics. I ran the Merida marathon twice, though I never came in first place, I greatly enjoyed running and crossing the finish line. I joined a boy scout troop because I loved hiking. I would choose nature over city situations that could lead to violence. I have always been thrilled by science.

When I was 15 years old, my parents paid my way to Chiapas. I was deeply impressed during my visit to the archeological site of Palenque; after that my mind went through a profound transformation. I started having dreams, visions like something was suddenly opening up in my head that made me understand my ancestors way of life as well as the depths of my grandfather's teachings. This increased my thrill for archeological sites.

I was never the same after that first trip. I could clearly feel the expansion of my consciousness resulting in a more elevated state of awareness. I then realized that everything was related to everything else, everything was bound to everything else; nothing was separate and, most importantly, I was able to interpret the ancients' messages that were engraved on the pyramids walls, the steles, the glyphs and the wall paintings. I realized that although our spiritual ancestors had been murdered during the conquest, and the pyramids plundered, my ancestors' original messages remained intact. All that was needed was to put the pieces together, like a puzzle, and interpret the messages left for us.

Today, the role my grandfather exerted in my early childhood makes total sense. My school education did not endow me with higher knowledge but it did imprint the neuron wiring in my brain that would open for me the door to the spiritual realm and planes of different frequencies. I shall explain this further in somewhat scientific terms.

Science states that after a human being is born, and during his early learning process (in childhood), his brain -containing more than 100 billion interconnected neurons- undergoes adaptive adjustment, thus shaping the human personality. The individual acquires beliefs at this stage and develops his own personal "style". This is known as "brain structure". It is, a way of looking at things and perceiving life, which is influenced by the family-social-environment in which we grow up. So one's life takes form according to how our brain was wired at an early age; this has an influence on our subsequent behaviors and our assimilation of ideas. For example, if you are born in Russia your language will be Russian; if you are born in a Christian family, you will believe in Christ; if you are born in a Buddhist family, you'll believe in Buddha. If you are born in a family who have love and respect for others, you'll find this later in life. If you are born in a dysfunctional family, you'll find similar conflicts as you grow up, and this is all due to your neuron brain wiring and the chemical processes that take place every time you produce a thought.

On the other hand, scientists have discovered that this can be changed; you have the capacity to change these early structures if you learn to control your thoughts. Thoughts have a strong influence on your personal ways and habits. Meditate, pray, think differently from what you were taught and you can replace the old structures for new ones that are more in accord with your current you. If you are living your life the way you like and you enjoy what you are doing, you have nothing to change, just enjoy who you are.

That's exactly what happened to me. I may not have been an outstanding student in the educational system, I may not have been endowed with a superlative intelligence, but what I did have was the capacity to be happy, to perceive life clearly and to connect myself to my ancestors, energetically. Some may consider this spiritual communication; I would just say it is a way of accessing a certain frequency created at a given moment back in time that has remained latent until now.

Scientists have discovered that water can capture and transmit information, that plants can respond to certain physical-chemical stimuli. Even though you may not know this, whenever you are thinking, you are sending forth a vibration frequency like a radio when it broadcasts signals out to the world, and that is why some times when you are thinking of someone, you bump into them on the street or they call you at that moment. What explains this is that we are all connected energetically; so just as different frequencies exist in our three dimensional reality, there are many other frequencies in other planes of reality. So I strongly encourage you to seek peace of mind and inner quiet, which means relaxing and quieting your mind. That way, you will perceive that your body is connected with everything around you. It's possible, then, to be in touch with the whole Universe, with everything and with everyone, because we are all one organism and nothing is separate from anything else.

Each neuron in your brain functions as an inter dimensional antenna that can capture different frequencies, not only of physical things and sounds, but of frequencies from the past, present and future.

Have you ever wondered why so many people have spiritual experiences? It is difficult to imagine someone who has never had a spiritual experience; for example, some times we hear someone calling us and we turn around and no one is there or suddenly we sense a shadow passing so swiftly by that we cannot tell who it was. Have you ever dreamed of someone who comes to say goodbye just before they die? Or sensed when a family member or friend was in danger or going through a very difficult moment? And women; blessed be women because they are the living proof that perceiving different frequencies is possible. We call it "woman's intuition". Think about this! Your brain is a "vibrating inter dimensional machine". Whew, what a name!

When my grandfather raised me, he knew all about these things, probably not under the scientific terminology that I am using, but in his own wisdom and in the wisdom of our ancestral lineage. My grandfather knew it was more important to structure my neuron net to perceive these frequencies than for me to absorb rather trivial information in the educational system. Conventional education does not develop spirituality that will be needed in the most important stages of people's lives, and in fact it can render people insensitive to these frequencies. I now understand why my grandfather did not mind my not getting high grades at school or my name never appearing on the honor roll. How wise grandparents are! Thanks to the brain structure I developed as a child I was able to realize that my ancestors had left us messages to be deciphered and revealed to mankind today.

After my trip to the archeological site of Palenque, there was a new strength that burned like a flame inside of me, at times, not letting me sleep. I could not interpret it nor share it with others because they might consider me crazy. I could sense something awesome was coming to me; the moment to reveal to the World about the Maya and their messages.

I barely finished secondary school. My parents tried to convince me to go to university so that I could become " somebody" but my inner voice told me that this was not my path. Instead, I had to strike out on my own and be responsible for myself, supported only by my "inter dimensional vibration machine", in other words, with my own brain structure.

I entered a technical school to learn how the Universe functions and picked out a profession where I could take subjects like: electronics, electricity, thermodynamics, calculus, mathematics, welding, minerals, colors, drawing, architecture, carpentry, design and more. I did not understand then why I felt so attracted to these subjects, they just thrilled me in one way or another, and this excitement was already working on my brain, creating new structures that would later help me understand and transmit my ancestors' messages in a scientific way.

When I finished my technical studies, I worked for some time in a local company in Merida, then I felt the need for another "time of silence" and inner quiet in order to synchronize my new brain structures. It took a great amount of energy for me to try and keep pace with something I had not yet grasped completely or understood, but that would later become my "mission".

I took my parents and siblings' advice and with their financial support started working for a recently nationalized company; the National Railroad Company. It was in that company that I became most aware of the lack of spirituality in the human being. It was there, that I became acquainted with the gross corruption in those environments. I understand now that it is pointless to have values and principles, when people are not going to put them into practice, and that life is more circumstantial than spiritual most of the time. Circumstances modify people's values and principles while the spiritual never changes. When you are a spiritual person, you know what is right and wrong. In the spiritual realm there is no real need for stated values and principles because there is balance and harmony. Consequently it is at peace. That is why, in spite of economic hardships, my father taught us never to take what did not belong to us. Such an attitude was in our lineage.

In the company I felt exploited when I encountered the trade union. I knew that if I wanted a "better" income I would have to "pay" for it, very costly for me and, at the same time, very profitable for the union leaders. I imagine many trade unions are like this (though they may not admit it). This all had a purpose: first it made me aware of the lack of spirituality of many workers; second: I became more physically fit because the tasks I did required physical strength; third: it opened my eyes to the misery and recklessness of humans: drugs, alcohol, prostitution and other disgraces that revealed people's suffering. I also observed that their faulty behavior put the life of other workers at risk.

So I just did my job the best I could. For a long time my mind was quiet and silent, even at peace. I was being prepared like an athlete who trains for a grand race, although I didn't know when the grand moment for me to take action would come. I decided to leave that up to life and to my ancestors.

And the day arrived. I was in the railroad's locomotive traveling together with some fellow workers; next to me was a young man who had joined the railroad at the same time I did. I remember him vaguely but a comment of his had a tremendous impact on me and triggered my "inter dimensional vibration machine" –my brain- into action again. We were heading to Campeche with empty oil tanks and we were to bring some filled ones back to the thermoelectric company in Merida city. The train followed course; I was standing in the locomotive cabin next to my co-worker; the other locomotive men were at their working posts. Suddenly, one of the conductors felt tired and decided to lie down on the floor, so I sat on the conductor's chair. I contemplated the never ending rail as it was "swallowed" by the train as it ran down the track. The track was lined on both sides by endless trees that seemed to run by in a parallel alignment. The scenario brought me into a meditative frame of mind; then, it all turned into total silence, like I was suspended up in space. Suddenly, my co-worker's voice broke the silence:

 " Hey buddy! "
 Then he added:
"I can't imagine you spending the rest of your life sitting there. You're different; you don't belong here. You were probably meant for something else. I don't see your future on the railroad!"

His comment exploded like thunder in my head, I could hear it over and over. After all these years, I still remember the tremendous impact his words had on me.

The train journey continued and we arrived in Campeche; we replaced the empty tanks for the filled ones and headed back to Merida, but on the way back I was not the same person. My inner flame was lit anew and more intensely so. I knew I wouldn't stay there any longer. I quit the job as soon as I found the opportunity. My family expressed their disappointment to me for my having left a job opportunity that had been gained with great pains and that had cost us so dearly. Their argument was I should not abandon that company because it paid better than others. However, they respected my decision. A few years later, the company closed.

Upon leaving the job I gathered my savings to tour the archeological sites in and around my native state. I could feel that old strong call inside of me; I was continuously surprised at the new things I saw. I made most of the journey by myself, but on that trip I met a foreign girl in the Mayan city of Coba. She was from Central America, of indigenous roots, but lived in Canada. She gave me a book and wrote me a very beautiful poem inside that spoke about freedom. Her poem was a sign that this time I was on the right track.

The Night of the Last Katún 2012 Maya

When I finished visiting the archeological sites near my native state , I felt like visiting other places. I went north to Monterrey and took a job with a company that trained people to make presentations, who then would go out and promote the company's products. I stayed there for a couple of years and learned about human relations and all about self esteem, until one day I decided to leave the company because they were not coming through with what they had promised. So I continued my path, knowing that I had received from that experience all that I had to learn.

When I first left the company I didn't really know what to do; I was on the street for several days without food or a bath, sleeping in parks without a clue as to what direction to follow. All I could feel was the cold winter approaching. It was early December; the cold was intense and I was not accustomed to it because temperatures never drop that low in Yucatan. The friends I had made in Monterrey had all left, so I was alone, with no money in my pocket. I knew that my family was worried because they had not heard from me, but I had no means to get in touch with them.

So I   decided to beg for money in the street to buy a phone card. Hearing from my family would be more nutritious to me than food itself, so as soon as I had the money, I bought a phone card and carried it with me like a treasure. On December 31st my family would get together in my parents' house to celebrate the New Year. When I was about to dial my home number, I had to gather strength because I knew it was going to be an emotional shock. My heart is still overwhelmed when I recall that moment.

Then I made up my mind and just dialed. My sister Yoli answered the phone. From the other side I heard her asking me how I was. She said my family wanted to see me, and asked me to come home because they were concerned about me. I don't know how, but I replied I was fine and not to worry about me. I told them to enjoy the treasured moments they shared together. Then they all gathered around the telephone and shouted in one voice: "Happy New Year!" My heart sunk and thick tears rolled down my cheeks. I managed to gather the strength to say

The Night of the Last Katún 2012 Maya

good bye, and then I hung up. I sat on the floor and cried my eyes out overcome by emotion, but I still didn't know what I was going to do. What I did know was that I was not going home; not then anyway.

Some mysterious force made me want to stay in Monterey, even when I had the opportunity of returning home right there in front of me. My family was so worried that one of my brothers in law, Alberto, who had traveled all the way up to Monterrey on a business trip, agreed to meet me at the Mall, on the day he arrived. When I saw him walking towards me, I felt very emotional, because he was the first family member I had seen in a long time. He tried to talk me into going back to Merida but, no matter how hard he tried to convince me , I said "no" because my intuition told me that something special was coming to me there.

After talking a while we said good bye; then I went back to roaming around the Mall where I was to spend the night. But happiness filled my heart because I had seen my brother in law, even if for such a short period of time. I was so excited I could hardly sleep that night. It must have been one or two o' clock in the morning and I was sitting on a bench when a well dressed man who seemed a bit drunk approached me and said:

" I see you've been around here for several days now, and I wish to ask you if you would rob a man like me?

I replied:
" I hadn't thought of it but even if I were in great need as I am now I wouldn't do a thing like that."

Then the man asked me if he could sit down with me. I shrugged my shoulders, so he sat down and his conversation went as follows. He spoke to me about the cosmos, the planet Venus, the suffering of human beings and God, and in a most peculiar way he told me that God was looking for someone who could make human beings know about the great power they have and are not using. After his rather long address he treated me to some hot dogs which I wolfed down in seconds because I hadn't eaten in several days. When we went back to the bench, he asked

26

me to kneel in front of him so he could pass me a secret to make very good money. His request made me burst into laughter. I told him I would never kneel in front of anyone, much less for money, that my race was proud not because of the money they had but for the spirituality they had developed. The man insisted on showing me his Rolex and the thick gold chains that hung from his neck and his huge rings, but he could not convince me. Then he just smiled and uttered:

" Be ready because someone is coming for you tomorrow."

I didn't pay much attention to his assertion, though it did seem a bit odd. So I just relaxed and sat there, dwelling upon the pleasurable memory of having seen my brother in law that day.

Spiritual experiences or revelations that we go through in our lives can come in human form and can appear in very concrete ways, so that we can grasp the messages as thoroughly as possible.

It was dawn and the morning was cold, but I had the intuition that something special was due to happen, and my heart beat strongly.

Before people started to circulate in the park, I decided to bathe and wash the clothes I was wearing in a fountain that was at the edge of the Mall park.. After washing, I hung my clothes to dry, under a street lamp that lit the garden. The cold was hard to bear so I climbed the light post seeking some warmth from the lamp.

When I realized that my clothes were almost dry, I put them on before people or a policeman would show up in the park. With my damp clothes on I waited for the first rays of the sun to strike, assuming it would warm me a bit. But I was wrong as mornings are still cold when the sun comes out. I was still damp so I ran towards a warm air outlet at a hotel nearby and stayed close to it until the sun rose. People started showing up in the Mall. I was happy wearing clean clothes. I sat and waited, and waited... Waited for what? I didn't know; I simply remained seated on my bench at the Mall watching time go by. Hours went by, but I didn't feel like leaving because I sensed something was due to happen.

Now the sun was setting; it was about six o'clock in the afternoon when I saw the silhouette of a person approaching me. It was a woman wearing a skirt down to her ankles; with sport shoes and a white blouse that covered her hands and neck. She had a dark complexion that I assumed was from a life in the sun.. She held a bucket full of flowers in her hand. She greeted me as she came near:

" Hello, my name is Gema, can I talk with you a while?"

" Sure " I said.(I didn't have much to do at that moment, except for waiting)

She sat down and after introducing herself informally, she proceeded to talk:

" Last night I dreamed I was talking with God and in that dream He asked me to come here and pick someone up."

"With God? to pick up who?" I replied.

She went on: "I had a vision of someone sitting on a bench exactly where you are, who looked exactly like you. I work in a movement for peace and I'm inviting you to come with me to our headquarters where you will learn about the history of humanity and the main religions of today, so you can become acquainted with our movement for peace around the world".

I felt that what Gema was telling me was exactly what I was waiting for, so I decided to go to with her to her office. From that day, the last stage of my training began: it involved general and spiritual knowledge which later helped me have a clearer vision of my ancestors' messages.

To make a long story short, I'll say that they taught me about Christianity as well as Buddhism; and about History and communism. I visited different cities and countries to develop within myself the spirituality that had to be activated in my "inter dimensional vibration machine" (my brain). After a few years of participating with the group for world peace, inner peace and religious unity, I decided to follow my own path because I felt I was now ready to understand and convey my ancestors' messages clearly and accurately.

I beg you dear reader, to withhold your judgment until you finish reading this book. I'm sure that if you do, you will wish to be part of the awakening of the super consciousness that will allow us to accept and respect each other and live together in peace and harmony.

II THE PIECES OF THE MESSAGE

The Night of the Last Katún 2012 Maya

1. The pieces of the message

One of the things that my grandfather used to tell me, was that people of my generation were going to live through a tremendous happening. This implied great responsibility from everyone because we were approaching the end of the era of unconsciousness and spiritual darkness. The event would begin with a planetary alignment that would increase the vibration of the Earth and diminish its magnetic field. The Earth would enter a new geological era; which would be a very auspicious moment for the return of our Mayan ancestors. He asked me to be ready to recognize *Hunab Ku,* (astronomical event that marks the beginning of a new consciousness on Earth). He added that I would know what to do in due time because he had trained me for the task.

I need to explain that *Maya* does not refer here to individuals coming from the Southeast of Mexico, but to people who've reached a state of awareness where they understand the synchronicity of the Universe and the connections bonding everything together, that one thing is not separate from the other. This Maya philosophy can be summarized by the assertion: "You are my other me".

Today, thanks to modern technology like television, Internet and the mass media, I can clearly see what my grandfather foretold. I observe daily the ever more evident changes on the planet, and I have come to the conclusion that we are reaching a point where humans' living in this state of unconsciousness and lack of harmony cannot go on for much longer.

The Night of the Last Katún 2012 Maya

My ancestors knew that the 1999 eclipse would unleash a new vibration on the Earth and on peoples' brains, thus, allowing for a new form of human consciousness which would prepare for the return of the Mayas. After the eclipse, humans' pineal gland was activated. This gland is responsible for the production of brain chemicals that allow access to a wider scope of perception and discernment over the things that damage us and those that bring us harmony and equilibrium. This is why after that astronomical event, our planetary awareness, our sense of unity and our yearning for a totally new lifestyle have increased, creating a greater need for peace of mind and spirituality .

2. *U' xooko' ob dzolkino' obo*
(Mayan calendar or time counter)

The Maya left us the U' xooko' ob dzolkino' obo (time counter or calendar as we now know it). The Mayan calendar stopped in 1992 when the last Katun (20 year period) began. From that day on, changes in the planet were intensified: the climate changes, the major and more frequent earthquakes, just to mention a few.. My grandfather had prophesied all of this when he told me of Hunab Ku's coming. Such changes would be the signs announcing the new era

The 1999 sun eclipse marked the arrival of *Hunab Ku*. The moon eclipse on the 16th of August, 2008 completed the cycle of the opening of the portal of light that heralded the beginning of the new consciousness based on unity, diversity and harmony.

Hunab Ku is the primal universal force representing the feminine and masculine principles –the duality- of God. This deity is symbolized by the two eclipses of the last *KaTun* (20 years that go from 1992 to 2012). The total sun eclipse of 1999 and the full moon eclipse in 2008 express the merging of the masculine (represented by the sun) and the feminine (represented by the moon) principal.
It also expresses the physical and the spiritual aspects of reality. What *Hunab Ku* symbolizes is equivalent to the Tao's yin and yang forces, representing the perfect balance of our dual Universe.

The Maya held that the pineal gland becomes more active after an astronomical event because the solar radiation and the moonlight both increase the brain's production of chemicals that alter human consciousness. They also knew that humans could not activate their pineal gland by themselves but had to wait for such events to take place and make it happen. The fact that we, as human beings, are more aware

The Night of the Last Katún 2012 Maya

today than we were ten years ago, aware that everything in the cosmos is interconnected, that we are all one and the same, that we are whole and part simultaneously, is not a random event. The Maya knew that it was up to humans to care and do something about our future. It is time we assume responsibility for change instead of just pretending or wishing that there be peace, without taking any steps in that direction. It is not possible for others to do our duty, but if each one assumes responsibility in this process of change, we will most certainly arrive in the year 2012 with a different mentality.

The *Maa yab* people made up the *Xook K'iinil* (calendar) not only to measure time but also to measure the solar winds, the Earth's warming and its influence on human's neuron activity. (consciousness). The calendar's main function is to measure human perception and provide the signals that will determine the exact moment when we must become actively responsible for change. The Maya were aware that time is infinite and could be counted to infinity, however, they left us a calendar up to the year 2012 to leave it to our generation to commence a new count, in the light of a new spiritual awareness.

3. U´ulab Ch´iha´an ula' ak´ Kín
(Encounter with my ancestors)

I met several visionaries during my spiritual instruction period, many of whom were regularly visited by our ancestors. They asked these sages to help me in my personal development, for me to continue my path and follow my cause. I learned that it was not a coincidence that I'd come to Earth. I was then clear to perceive why I felt different from others; it was because I was born with a mission. From that moment on, I could readily understand things around me; everything seemed to make sense and I was able to perceive people's energy and the energy of things and the elements. I understood that I came to Earth to wake people up and tell them who they really are, where they are going and how they can reach their destination.

Many years after my spiritual training had begun, I felt the enormous need to visit Merida city, but it was not until 1996 that I was able to go back. The reunion with my family   was so incredibly emotional that those moments remain forever in my memory and encourage me to continue my mission. A few weeks after my arrival, I was eager to transmit my first message because I wanted to promote people's self-
esteem and wanted them to discover their inner power. So I decided to give my first lecture.

A couple of months later, Carmen arrived in Merida. This woman is from Aztlan descent. She was my travel companion and one with whom I shared numerous spiritual expansion experiences. She became like my "spiritual eyes" and, in many ways, my spiritual guide because she often, with great patience, elucidated the spiritual messages I could not understand. So I entrusted her my thoughts on how I was planning to give my lectures and workshops.

She asked me if I had worked out the contents of my program, and I explained to her that I had become aware of my ability to perceive people's energy when they're in front of me and thus I couldn't follow a given program, since each person is different and understands things in their own way. So I decided to give my lectures without planning them in advance, only anticipating the general topics to be covered, which were basically related to self esteem and the power within. I asked Carmen to give me a hand at this and to ask the spiritual beings what name I should give to my workshops. It took some days to get the answer.

Before Carmen notified me about the workshop's name, she informed me that the name revealed to her was going to have great impact on people's vibration frequency and would bring many people to the event. The title was "I AM" and, just as she had anticipated, we gave more than 30 workshops with that name that helped many find their path to freedom.

One of the most gratifying experiences I can recall -from the hundreds of people I met in those workshops- took place as I was walking on Paseo de Montejo –Merida's main avenue-. An 18 to 20 year old girl came up to me and said that the most precious thing that had happened in her life had been to attend the "I Am" lecture. I asked her who she was, and she said I would not remember because there were so many people in my workshops. I asked her to give me a hint, and she insisted I would not remember her, but that I might recall a girl who didn't have money to pay for the lecture. I immediately remembered who she was and told her that when she asked me to please let her in, I had noticed her low energetic field and felt happy to let her in for free. She then said that as she saw me walking in the street she felt compelled to come and thank me for the workshop, because on the day of the lecture she was feeling so depressed that she was contemplating suicide, and the workshop had changed her state of mind.

I've had many similar experiences that have filled me with great satisfaction.

Carmen and I worked tirelessly those years giving lectures and workshops. In the year 1998 we had a daughter who is from Aztlan and Maya descent. Our daughter's DNA carries the information of two great cultures, and we've taken great care to raise and guide her on the path of the new awareness. She's our precious jewel.

Carmen and I had to part for various reasons; she went to live in Tlaquepaque in Guadalajara, with our three year old daughter, while I explored various places in the states of Yucatan, Campeche and Chiapas.

Two years passed without my seeing Carmen, although we talked regularly on the phone. I suggested she come for a vacation in Merida so I could see my daughter. So mother and child came and spent some leisure days with me, but when they were due to return to Guadalajara, something unexpected happened: to our surprise, our five year old daughter decided to stay and live with me. And this is how I became a 24 hour father for approximately a year. I shall cherish the beautiful memories of those days for the rest of my life.

I was enjoying my daughter's company one day when I had a most intense spiritual experience. It represents the beginning of the "light messages" revealed to me by my ancestors to lead humanity to a totally new way of life.

It was just before dawn and I was sitting in the living room of our rented house in Merida. I was not sleepy so I took to reflecting about life, love, couples, the economy and the human way of life. I was deep into thought because I couldn't understand why human relations are so strange, with no sense of unity whatsoever. In a world with wars, famine, unhappiness, poverty, etc; how can man still consider himself "intelligent? ". This confused me. Man has even devised a scale to measure his intelligence: the famous "IQ" test. I personally believe intelligence should be measured in terms of happiness, and so should spirituality. The IQ standard only measures man's intelligence as a collection of abilities to integrate information.

I began to wonder if knowledge was really available to all of those who seek it. Why can't human beings be prepared to live a life of harmony, peace and happiness?   As I sat there caught in deep thought, I contemplated the beauty of Creation at night.   It was about four o'clock in the morning; the moon was still high in the night sky. The light of the full moon shone over things with a special glow.   It was a mystical dawn, and next to the moon was the large star that had kept me company since I was a little boy.. That "bright star" –as grandpa used to call it- was non other than the planet Venus (*L'amat*). Together with the moon, it shone intensely that night, announcing that something was about to happen.

My grandfather used to say that when the moon was full and the "bright star" shone intensely it would be an excellent night to go out to the patio and have our bodies showered by the combined beams of the moon and Venus, for our body's energy to become balanced and for us to experience harmony within ourselves and with all the beings around us. So I went out to the patio to admire and receive the moon and the "bright star's" rays on my body, as I used to do as a child with my grandfather.

Half an hour must have gone by when I heard the door open and a sweet and tender voice say:

" Papi... what are you doing?"

It was my little girl who had awakened. I took her in my arms and we sat on the chair together to admire the energetic night, and I told her about the things I had learned from my grandfather. I told her about the "bright star" Venus and how we'd named her after that star, because Venus in the Mayan language is L'AMAT: "the key element of our culture" and the foundation upon which the Mayas built their astronomical knowledge. The name has such profound meaning I thought it would be suitable for our daughter because she's such an alert child. Our parental guidance must preserve her spiritual nature to keep her growing in good balance and synchrony with the Universe.

The upbringing my daughter was going to receive from me involved the command of her emotions and her mind. Since I had been trained in those aspects of the art of living, it was up to me to pass this knowledge down to her. What I didn't know then was that she would also teach me

The Night of the Last Katún 2012 Maya

a great many things.

Every child is born with the capacity to contact the spiritual world, as I shall explain later, when I teach you a meditation and visualization technique. With the techniques I'd learned from my grandfather, I was communicating with my ancestors on the patio one day, when the connection to the spiritual realm became clear to me; especially in regards to children. Children perceive the subtle realities that have a life parallel to our Universe. As adults we never pay attention to those matters. When children dare talk about what they see, adults even tell them to shut up and stop imagining things. Their attitude comes from ignorance and, most of all, fear. But then, who doesn't become afraid when they feel they're being touched by some intangible being or sense an invisible presence next to them?

Although we are born with perception, as we grow up and become "adults" we forget and become disconnected, wrapped up in daily conflicts –with love partners, the economy, wars, disasters, etc.- to the point where we forget the most essential thing: our spiritual awareness. However, children's innocence is still intact, they're still connected to the spiritual world and, most of all; they are consciously in touch with God. With this preface I begin this marvelous account that I wish to share with you for the sake of your awakening, the relationships with your partner, your family and your work. The focus here is on spiritual freedom.

Here's what happened that morning:

My daughter and I were still sitting on the patio, admiring the night beauty when suddenly we heard noise coming from the living room, like footsteps in the darkness. The room was empty because I had adapted it as a small lecture hall. A Mayan leather parchment hung down the wall; it had been given to me by the Maya people in Palenque. The pyrographed painting showed the enthronement (ceremony where command is handed down to a descendant) of the last king *Chan Bahlum*, son of *Pakal Kin*. I thought a cat might have sneaked into the house, so we tried to get in carefully to throw it out, but when I tried getting in I realized the door was closed, so it was impossible for a cat or any other animal to have gone in. I peeped in through a window to see whether the door to the street was open to discard the possibility of someone having broken into the house. But it was firmly closed. After I made sure the house was empty, I carried my little girl into the house, and as I did, she made a comment:

"Look daddy, my king came down!"

She was referring to King *Chan Bahlum* that was represented in the parchment drawing. It was not that the king had come down or out of the picture. *L'amat* told me that her king, as she used to call him, had always been with her since the day she was born and also with me. In fact, throughout the years, the seers I've come in touch with, have always told me they see a man next to me, escorting me, who has the appearance of a Mayan king. I have sensed the presence and seen this noble character on several occasions, although my perception is not as accurate as my daughter's.

In the darkness, the faint silhouette of a tall and rather robust man with an eagle nose, emerged. He was wearing a cloak that covered his body from shoulders to knees and was adorned with jade necklaces and thick bracelets. He wore a *copilli* (headdress) made of Quetzal feathers. King *Chan Bahlum* was standing in front of us, with a patient but firm expression, showing sadness and compassion at the same time. There we stood, the three of us looking at one another without saying a word. We were –rather I was- stunned by the circumstances. How would you have felt in my place in such an awesome situation? After a few minutes that seemed like hours, the king gave me the following message that I will now pass on to you just as it was given...

"We have thoroughly guided you since you were born until today. Now the time has arrived for you to become the receptor and bearer of our messages to our descendants. We are thankful to you for having given us a child from the Aztlan-Mayan descent. -*L'amat Itzel*- who carries in her the essence of our lineage. This will motivate you to defend the way of life of the Maya and the Aztlan cultures that have unfortunately been so disfigured. Thanks to your grandfather -*Ahau Tah Huchin*- who developed your neuron wiring- and to your daughter's higher energetic connection, we are able to communicate with you. My father *Pakal Kin*, together with other Mayan leaders, wishes to reveal their knowledge directly to you, and they have asked me to transmit their messages . They will correct your conceptions about the Maya and help you change completely our people's customs and habits.The time has come for a totally new way of life."

This is how he described the Maya people :

"The Maya was a culture of advanced thinkers and technological people who were pacifists as well, and who were devoted to inner peace and spirituality. The Maya were also intelligent and evolved individuals who had the ability to interpret nature and the astronomical phenomena. It is not true that the Maya practiced human sacrifices to worship their *Seen Kin* (gods). In reality, we did not have many gods as is commonly believed. We saw *Hunab Ku* everywhere and felt a part of Him, which is a totally different thing. We had a clear vision that everything is linked to God and the Universe, and we tried to transmit the idea that the Universe is part of you and you are part of it. We are all part of the whole. Here's what I have to say in that respect…"

I was captivated as the noble character continued talking:

"What is known today as Mexico is the place to begin the renovation and awakening of a new awareness. Mexico has the adequate energetic conditions for this purpose. The atmosphere for change has been prepared for hundreds of years, a new history must be written and nothing will stop it from happening, provided people awaken and assume their responsibility. People have lost track completely. The values and principals upon which you base your civilization are never respected because your lives are vain and circumstantial, the quality of life is inappropriate, people are unhappy in general, there is too much resentment in people's hearts, there is too much corruption and abuse of power in society, and people seem to be overwhelmed with moral sickness everywhere.

The Night of the Last Katún 2012 Maya

No one trusts anyone else, people's houses are surrounded by iron gates, making themselves prisoners. You have filled your houses with perishable and valueless items, but most of all, you've caused great damage to Nature, you have plundered your environment: the oceans, the rivers, the forests, everything!

What kind of life are you leading? You don't know what love is. Your wealth is built over the lessening and exploitation of others, you take advantage of their ignorance, disregarding that there could be abundance for all. Imbalance prevails, power only serves the illicit enrichment of a few; your economic system makes the poor even poorer. You are not in control of your emotions, and you end up hurting other people. Your focus is on having beautiful houses, automatic devices in which to get in and ride at great speed, with no regard to the responsibility it implies, and because you have no control of the exerted energy, you often cause damage. (accidents). Family decay is increasing, passing down great frustration and resentment to the children, who are so totally misguided by the concept of freedom that they take to doing whatever comes to their mind, with no regard for consequences. Disputes among siblings and between parents and children get harsher all of the time. People get sicker and new diseases crop up every day, affecting many innocent people. Is this really living?

The time has come for all of those who are receiving these messages to assume responsibility and start putting them into practice to form "the new enlightened race with the children of the new spiritual consciousness."

The king explained further:

"So as there are physical laws like:: gravity, atmospheric pressure, fluid pressure, lineal timing, etc., there are spiritual laws that have a relationship with the physical world, and if these laws are trespassed, it produces imbalance and suffering to those who still live on the physical plane. The great majority of people who are part of your era have trespassed them!. A good example of this is what happened in Mexico

The Night of the Last Katún   2012 Maya

during the conquest lead by Hernan Cortes in 1519, which murdered hundreds of thousands of indigenous people in the name of God; and then pillaged the archeological sites they had founded. The vibration frequency of resentment, deep pain and unhappiness was born, which has lasted until today and must be neutralized for these people to evolve. Observe how they live today: everything is about mistrust, robbery, violence, etc. Something must be done urgently, not just becoming aware of it and not doing anything".

Finally, he said:
"You will be receiving information in different ways for several days, for example, through conversations that the Mayan kings (spiritual beings) will have with you. You must write it down in the terms that people of your Era can understand. Keep it simple; modern humans like to complicate their existence too much".

After that conversation, my daughter fell asleep in my arms and when I took her to bed and came back to the living room, the spiritual presence of the last Mayan king had disappeared. Several days went by, before I was given more information. I knew that the task I had ahead of me was hard, but that I was not alone in it.

To assimilate information more clearly, I visited a Mayan shaman who lived on Playa del Carmen in the state of Quintana Roo state, on the Mexican Caribbean, to receive an energetic cleansing. He explained to me that part of the low frequency energy of the people I had dealt with in my life -mainly those whom I had helped with energetic therapy- had remained in me, blocking my energy flow, thus, hindering my spiritual clarity which I needed to receive the messages.

We see that historic events are cyclical; our generation is facing a process of change and the end of an Era. All of us have a role in this change. Sooner or later everyone will assume the new way of life, in spite of people's disbelief, mistrust and corruption of modern societies. These are the facts we are facing. I assume full responsibility for all of my actions. God and the higher teachers willing, I shall become a good messenger of their knowledge.

The Night of the Last Katún 2012 Maya

Several days had gone by since the kings first visit, then one night, while I was meditating, I had the first revelation through an astral voyage; it was similar to when you dream that you're flying but you're completely lucid at the same time. I was transported to a Mayan city called *Uxmal* –an archeological site in Yucatan state-. It has a hall called "the Monk Quadrangle". It includes different chambers located around a central patio. Several spiritual beings welcomed me there and gave me the following teachings:

"For the world to reach equilibrium, two things are required: the feminine and the masculine principles. The Mayan city of *Uxmal* represents the feminine principle because it relates to your inner nature, you inner "I", your consciousness. That is why "The Sorcerer's Temple" -the only oval pyramid here- was built with no angles. When you experience your full consciousness, you can relate to everyone without affecting them. You must seek balance between the spiritual realm and the physical world, to avoid falling in the grip of human weakness and egotism.

"This city was built for the education of spiritual leaders and shamans who served the king, and for the king himself. In this place, they met their essential "I" and harmonized their inner being, to become incorruptible and loyal servers of the people, but also to become prosperous and bearers of abundance to their people and families. In this place, they reached the capacity to manifest total harmony and equilibrium. Here, they sat for long periods of time to think, meditate and plan, observe and analyze, in order to expand their awareness."

"To be a conscious individual means to become aware of your actions and be able to control them when you know they hurt you or go against humanity. The current generations have developed the sickness of "ego" and this, together with power, is leading humans to their own extinction, because they've lost focus of what is more crucial today: the global warming of the Earth. We left our visions and astronomical calculations for our descendants, but this legacy was destroyed almost completely when the new race arrived in these lands. However, it was very

The Night of the Last Katún 2012 Maya

fortunate that your grandparents remained faithful to their spiritual legacy, and that is why we are able to communicate with you today and to put our astronomical knowledge in your hands. For centuries, we tried to guide humans. We were evolved beings and wished to pass on our knowledge. Humans are so egocentric and unruly and they have brought their own Era to a complete decay."

I then interrupted him with a question:

"If you did evolve, how come you did not take into consideration the fact that our generation (our Era) was going to suffer the oppression and ravage of the conquest, and the massive destruction of the high knowledge contained in your sacred parchments?"

They replied:
"When we evolved we knew that individuals of low energy could come and destroy the valuable knowledge we were leaving you, as indeed happened. The ignorant have a tendency to destroy the things they cannot understand. Because we knew this, we left you valuable information in different forms, that would survive in spite of what was to be annihilated. The true legacy of the Maya is in the pyramids, in the steles. The information is everywhere for you to use and carry out a revolution of consciousness. But we come back to where we started: you lost track and whatever you don't use, you lose. It's a fact that the conquerors ravaged and destroyed the knowledge we had left you, but the essential remains intact. People in this Era ceased to evolve; they are worse off now than at the beginning of the Era. The course of their civilization has only fostered poverty, death, loneliness. Just look around you and see all the misery that exists. People are unable to draw lessons from their past history; in fact, they use their past history as an excuse to justify their poor existence today. They use their past to place blame for the misery of their current lives."

Then they added:

"Consciousness means responsibility. If one does not take responsibility for one's actions, one can not evolve. Here (meaning in the Monk

The Night of the Last Katún 2012 Maya

Quadrangle inside of the Sorcerer's Temple), the future spiritual guides (shamans, kings) are granted visions of how they are to use the given knowledge, to be elevated from an individual level onto a cosmic level. Here is where they come to grips with change; they learn from their past experiences as well as from the lives of spiritual leaders that preceded them, and acquire the wisdom to follow their current personal process."

Then I asked him how we could create this new consciousness?

"Only through knowledge and the relationship with others can you eventually reach unity. We are at the dawn of an energetic-spiritual revolution, of a new consciousness, a new way of life, one where you can fall in love and experience authentic passion for what you do. If you cannot feel this it is because you have ceased to evolve and you have fallen into the abyss of ignorance. Evolution is all about emotion, passion, joy, happiness, energy and love. If humans cannot experience this, they are dead men walking, and they'd better get down to searching for the true meaning of their lives.

Many people believe that taking their lives will put an end to their suffering, but it only makes it worse. Yet, this is not up to me to teach you; you shall learn about this later. My role here is to make you aware of true life, a life with abundance, passion, joy and energy. It is important that people do the things that they like; while they can still do them; it will be too late when they are too tired to change. Change while you feel young, strong, vigorous, energetic and curious. If you wish to evolve, you must modify your way of life, your beliefs (the limiting ones that is), and your values. Everything must evolve, otherwise you are no more than a pack of fearful people –and the world is full of them-.

People have grown physically but not mentally or spiritually. They feel threatened by the same fears they had before; they are afraid of change, of being different, of being considered crazy; they fear criticism; they don't dare go beyond their safety limits. They are comfortably living in the nothingness, their well known fears, and their angst. They are so alienated, they can close their eyes to the dismal injustice around them.

The Night of the Last Katún 2012 Maya

They live in constant disagreement with their love partners, they accumulate energy in their heads without knowing what to do with it. They are "neurotic" individuals; they put up with verbal and physical aggression from their spouses. Many people in your era are afraid of *Hunab Ku*; they follow the creeds and values they were fed in childhood, they are afraid of expressing their true feelings and emotions; they are afraid of being themselves and are afraid of making mistakes, of failing, of not being good enough."

They also stressed the following:

"Evolution comes with change. When you grow up, your clothes don't fit anymore and you must get new ones, likewise, when you evolve, your old integrity doesn't suit you anymore, and you must acquire a new level of integrity. And that's the purpose of one's past, to create new states of awareness, new standards of integrity. As the evolving beings that you are, you must take responsibility for your actions. To help you realize this, I am going to reveal one of the major discoveries that we left you. You will then understand where we come from. We left you one of the most obvious landmarks. I will soon take you there."

Right then, my mind cut away from that trend of thought. It was already 6 o'clock in the morning when my daughter's voice took me out of my daydream. She had to get ready to go to school, so she called me as soon as she'd opened her eyes. Going to school was enjoyable for her because she was learning to read and write which would allow her to tell her own stories and read all of the books she wanted in the future.

She was so eager to learn she copied everything I did. One day I was distracted and didn't see what she was doing to the illustrations I had prepared for my talk that day. She wrote underneath every one of my sentences, the same sentences! I feel moved whenever I observe a child being so thirsty to learn, because it makes me realize how important it is for us as adults to guide the innocent children in the right direction. I saw my little girl evolving spontaneously. I got her dressed and we left the house. On our way to her school, thoughts about the higher knowledge I had just received revolved in my mind.

The Night of the Last Katún 2012 Maya

Seldom do we stop to observe the events that take place around us. That day I saw parents yelling at their children to hurry up or because they'd made some mistake. There was extreme misery all around me, needy people who didn't have enough to eat or a place to sleep, people who had lost hope, given up on their dreams, and had resigned themselves to the little they had. Although they complained all the time, they barely did anything to change their fate. I became more keenly aware of the things I had learned. I felt an urgency to do something for them. I wanted to assume responsibility for the changes that were needed in the world.

Approximately fifteen days had gone by since my last spiritual experience. I had done some research on the matter to complete the information I needed. I had interviewed several people to hear their experiences, and I sensed that when they read this message, they would find their own path. I was ready to receive more revelations from the spiritual realm, so I asked two of my friends to join my daughter and me for a quick visit to the archeological site of Uxmal. It was Sunday, the sun shone brightly and it was a very hot day. But there I was, waiting for something outside of the ordinary to pop up or for some sign to appear. We had been in the place for about three hours when my little girl grabbed me by the hand and told me her king had asked her to take me to the city of light or sun city, in the direction of Campeche. We left at once for the archeological site of *Oxkintok* –"city of the three suns", from the root *ox*, meaning "three", *kin*, meaning "sun" and *tok*, which means "flint stone", due to the brightness of the local stones.

The archeological site was about to close when we arrived, so we begged the guard to let us in promising that we would not take long. He let us in because my young daughter was with us. We climbed the main pyramid where we saw stone effigies of beings wearing vests and woven sashes symbolizing strength, power, leadership and protection, who lay there as guardians of the place. There were no people there at the moment, but we could feel a strange vibration as though the place were crowded. We perceived what seemed to be shadows passing swiftly near us. It made our skin get goose bumps. The place was

The Night of the Last Katún 2012 Maya

brimming with energy. Then I asked my friends to wait for me down below while I went up the pyramid with my daughter. When we reached the top, there was a peculiar character waiting for us.

He was tall, had tan skin; wore golden pectoral pieces and cuff pieces of the same material. A headdress made of ocellated royal peacock feathers adorned his head. He bowed to us the oriental way and we returned the reverence in the same fashion. He then proceeded to tell us why we were in *Oxkintok*.

He said:
"We brought you to the city of *Oxkintok* –city of the three suns- because the solar energy that pours out of these stone pyramids will increase your vibration frequency and balance out your body energy; it will expand your awareness -through the activation of your pineal gland- so you can receive the most important message we have for your generation. It will help them change their concepts about life and become truly spiritual, but above all, to help them become individuals who wish to assume responsibility for their environment. The expansion of consciousness is a process that requires great amounts of energy in the form of heat, it helps to build new connections in your brain and in your body structure. Just remember, whenever we think you need to increase you molecular vibration, we shall ask you to take a sunbath. For now, just stay here a while, watching the sunset with your daughter and when you leave, don't bathe for the following 24 hours until your energy alignment has been completed."

After our brief visit to the city of *Oxkintok*, we went back to Merida at night. On our way back, we could feel a very smooth and agreeable energy. I was certain that every time I visited an archeological site, something was rewired inside of me that would help me decipher my ancestors' messages more clearly.

On the way back, my daughter told me that the day she saw "her king", he had given her a box with three little lights inside that represented the messages they wanted to reveal to me, so my task now was to decipher the messages.

49

III FIRST MESSAGE OF LIGHT

1. Yemeno' ob te kin' o
(We came down from the sun)

After a few weeks of daily activities I went back to the Mayan archeological sites. First, I visited my native village to say hello to one of my sisters, Lina, and her husband José. During my visit I went to *Ek Balam* (jaguar star) with my nephew, since it's only 30 minutes away from Espita (my native village). There, I had the following experience:

I was standing in front of the main temple, looking at the enormous plumed serpent that lay at the main entrance of the pyramid, when I saw many engravings and steles showing the history of the place and the purpose for which it was built. My eye was caught by a winged character like an angel, that really puzzled me because these kinds of sculptures appear only in this place.

Later I learned that the archeological site had been prepared as the abode for the guardians of my lineage, and symbolized the power that was never passed on but had returned to the spiritual realm. and which now has to come back from the spiritual realm to the physical world. And it was going to happen precisely in this place. That's why the serpent was surrounded by winged beings symbolizing the new consciousness coming through spiritual revelations. It also represented the approximate birth date of a royal descendant, who must come to wake up the *Maa yab* people (the chosen ones) to a more spiritual, harmonious and balanced consciousness based on unity.

I sat to meditate at length and this is what I envisioned:
As soon as I closed my eyes, my grandfather, *Ahau Tah Huchim* -who had transcended to the spiritual realm years before- appeared in front of me. He looked just as I remembered him, with his innocent smile –his trademark- he bowed the oriental way. It surprised me and I asked him why he did it. He replied it was a way to show gratitude and respect for one's descendants. He told me he - together with others from our lineage- had always been with me during my learning process, and on all the trips I had made. I felt honored and responded in the same

51

oriental way. He continued "talking" (talking is not the right term, because in the spiritual world there is no physical voice, but it's how I can explain how my grandfather was transmitting his messages to me through images.) He said the following:

"I'm happy that you have practiced what I've taught to you. You will get much benefit out of it; just keep your curiosity alive and be open to the signs you receive. Several spiritual beings are with me today because we must give you a crucial message that will change modern people's perception of life. Open your eyes and observe the entrance guarded by the winged beings. Sit on the small platform in front of it, and don't worry about the watchmen; they won't bother you."

He mentioned this because sitting on that platform is not allowed. Then he continued his address:

"The ancient Maya sensed that their descendants' awareness would decline to such a low level that they would not be able to understand the ancient messages, had they transmitted them in a complex way. So they used logic and simplicity, but until now, people have not been able to understand them. The ancestors feared that people's ignorance would lead to misunderstanding of the Mayan culture, and it did. Many in modern society think of the Maya as a savage, ignorant and blood thirsty crowd that worshiped many gods. But this is not true. Everything at the archeological site has a reason; just relax and open up your mind but, most of all, your heart. We -your ancestors- have been waiting for this crucial moment to arrive; it is meant to lead to the spiritual awakening of humanity."

I then stopped meditating and went to sit in the place my grandfather had indicated. The sun rays beat down on my skin, but my curiosity was stronger than the heat burning me. I sat on the platform with my legs crossed, focused on the entrance of the pyramid. The high temperature made me lethargic, but I fought the dullness and perked up, recovering my concentration. My grandfather appeared again and explained:

"Don't worry about the sun's striking rays and the temperature. These conditions are necessary to obtain this spiritual experience. Your neurons must reach a rather high vibration frequency for you to reach a higher level of perception."

I stopped paying attention to the heat and concentrated on what I was doing. After a few minutes, my range of perception grew wider and I was then able to perceive more spiritual beings around me, attired in elegant, colorful costumes, with flint necklaces and feathers ornamenting their clothing. *Ahau Tah* –one of the last rulers of *Ek Balam, Ahau Itzá*, governor of *Chichen Itzá* and *Ahau Pakal*, governor of Palenque, presented themselves to me. The three of them alluded to their rank and introduced themselves as Kululk'an Quetzalcoatl.

All of a sudden, I felt confused and happy at the same time: first, I felt happiness, because my grandfather's teachings proved to be real; second, I felt confused, because what I had read in textbooks was that *Kukulk'an and Quetzalcoatl* were different gods, who were worshiped through the sacrifice of virgins, and deeply revered by their subjects, in different places.

They observed me in awe and laughed at my thoughts, which confused me even more. They told me they could perceive my thoughts, and that they were no more than fantasies coming out of a horror story. Such stories were told by the conquerors themselves to make the people forget their own culture. This is how they covered up the murders, rape and genocide that they had perpetrated against the Mayan people. They made up stories that the Mayan gods and kings were gratified by human sacrifices as offerings. But the real truth about the many corpses found in the *cenotes* (caverns under water) is not that they were victims of sacrifice, but were people who had killed themselves when they were trapped in the siege of barbaric, non spiritual assailants. That is why they threw themselves into the *cenotes* before being raped and tortured. So the bodies of the women and children that were supposedly sacrificed at the archeological sites, were rather the victims of the barbaric slaughter perpetrated by the conquerors.

When the spiritual beings pronounced this, their smiles faded and their faces became serene. I then asked about Diego de Landa and his accounts about the Maya. To which they commented:

"It is a pity that the latter generations believed his stories; the conquerors didn't come to preach the gospel to the "Indians", but rather to despoil and enslave them, and to overpower them in the name of God, including Diego de Landa. Although the conquerors felt a certain respect for him, they did to the indigenous people what they pleased without taking his opinion into consideration, and Landa allowed this in order to take advantage of the pillage as well. He wrote a convenient story that distorted the facts concerning our people, thus creating a History that diverges from reality. We hold no resentment against anyone, we just want the world to recover its spirituality.

"Unfortunately, his version of Mayan history is the one that became known. People cannot see what they don't already have inside, and if they continue to believe those stories, they will continue to write the same things. If you want to see something different, you must have a good heart and true curiosity for the truth. That is why you were raised in a special way, and you were educated by people of our pure lineage. You are the last of the awakened Mayas. Your DNA contains our true History. Your grandfather, *Ahau Tah Huchin*, knew it. We have transmitted valuable information from generation to generation to preserve our history. That is why your grandfather raised you in a way that would keep your mind free from modern contamination in a world with no spiritual life or light. So assume your responsibility and tell them the true history!"

After saying this, they began their account. They said that many years ago, the vibration frequency of the Earth changed and, consequently, humans lost their spiritual vision, even the *Maa Yab* people who had been educated to take the evolutionary process forward. Their vibration frequency was so low that they lost their knowledge; well, not that they lost it but their brain did not have enough energy to interpret the information correctly. Then our ancestors picked out some of the *Maa Yab* lineages to transmit their knowledge through a variety of spiritual practices such as: contemplating nature, meditating, speaking in metaphors and, most of all, leading simple and peaceful lives. This allowed them to maintain the energetic level required to preserve the energetic chain of that elevated frequency.

I then understood why my grandfather didn't like to go to the city, and the few times he did he came back immediately. In fact, he was a loner, which was typical of most *Espitans* (from my native town, Espita). This personality trait helped them keep their brain energy high. The facts about my childhood then became clear to me; I also understood why I'd been sent to my grandfather's house at a very early age, and why I had been such a quiet boy during my childhood and adolescence. I understood why I felt different from the other kids; it was because I felt connected to everything in the world.

As I contemplated the pyramids, glyphs and steles, I could seize their meaning effortlessly, and that is exactly what the ancestors wanted. That is the reason why they had left engraved messages and codified information all over the archeological sites. The first step would be getting to understand the Maya concept of God, for this would shed light concerning our relationship with the Universe and with other human beings and would help us feel more connected to them. For my learning to be completed, I had to go to *Tulum* city in the state of Quintana Roo.

When the spiritual beings finished giving me this message, they, and my grandfather, took their leave ceremoniously. I instantly understood why the Mayan kings had introduced themselves as *Kukulk'an Quetzalcoatl*, because they were the highest in awareness among our people. I also understood that *Ek Balam* was the site where the new *Kululk'an Quetzoalcoatl* was to be born. I opened my eyes and stretched out my legs. I was perspiring profusely because the place was extremely hot. I took my time to recover. Then, one of my nephews showed up and prompted me to leave, for they'd explored the entire place and wanted to bathe in a *cenote* nearby. I got up swiftly and we left Ek Balam.

When we came back to *Espita*, we ate like kings. My sister Lina cooked turkey with "black stuffing" for us. It's a rather hot stew made of dry

The Night of the Last Katún 2012 Maya

chili roasted with coal, and macerated to give the dish its unique flavor. It's one of my favorite dishes so that day I had "black stuffing" for lunch and for dinner, and the next day, I had some more for breakfast. You will love this special dish when you taste it.

Early the next day, I headed to the beach of *Tulum*. Imagine yourself in front of the open sea on the Mexican Caribbean. From this vantage point, the sea typically takes on turquoise blue hues. The sand is so white that it reflects the sunlight brightly. It's so beautiful it enraptures you. The marine landscape brings you into a deep meditative state almost automatically.

It did it with me. When I was sitting in the shade next to a pyramid, marveling at the sight, I heard someone whispering in my ear... *Yemeno' ob' te kin' o* (We come from the sun). I was about to decipher the first message of light engraved on the pyramids!

On the front of the pyramid that I'm talking about, you can see an engraving known as the "Descending God". It represents someone in a descending position, wearing a jade pectoral piece and a headdress; he has a scepter in his hands, and his body shows embossed figures representing the sun. But what does this all mean? I will give you a metaphor as an explanation, and later I will make a comparison between this and humankind, because it is easier for the brain to understand when we have a reference point. The metaphor I'll use is the process of metamorphosis.

The Night of the Last Katún 2012 Maya

The story begins with the caterpillar, a chubby little animal with very slow movements. The caterpillar eats the leaves from which it gets the nutrients that it will need to change. After satisfying its hunger, it crawls up a tree for shelter, to build its cocoon. It then secretes a sticky liquid to shape it, adding layer over layer completely encasing the little animal.

The caterpillar remains static inside the cocoon, its molecules are slowly moving inside until one day they reach a totally new structure. It's the same energy it had originally but organized in a different way. Later, the caterpillar's mouth develops little tool-like pliers that help it get rid of the cocoon walls, almost molecule by molecule, until it breaks through. Then, a caterpillar with wings emerges! At first, the butterfly's wings are folded against its body but with the wind, they become hardened, enabling it to fly. The process is incredibly interesting if you think about it.

Now I ask you, who ate the leaves, the caterpillar or the butterfly? The answer is simple –you might say- the caterpillar ate them, and your answer would be correct. Or, the butterfly ate them, and your answer would also be correct. If you say it was the caterpillar before it became a butterfly, your answer would be correct too. If you say, it was the butterfly when it was still a caterpillar, it would also be right. The animal coming out of the cocoon is a butterfly -as we know it- but we might as well consider it still a caterpillar because that's the animal that went in. We can see it like a butterfly that cannot fly yet (before metamorphosis); or like a caterpillar that can fly (after metamorphosis). Considering it a caterpillar is fine because we're talking about the same animal, except it has a different look. I wish to make the metaphor's message totally clear because it is the very basis for understanding our own nature.

If we analyze the process carefully we will see that: the caterpillar in the cocoon has rather limited movements and activity. In that respect –from a physical, not ethical point of view- we could consider the caterpillar "inferior" to the butterfly. For a period of time, the energy and physical body of the caterpillar are transformed inside the cocoon so at the end of the process a "superior" animal will come out, that is, an animal with a much wider potential to do things, to span distances and do it faster, to soar to great heights, to obtain different kinds of food, etc. But if you think about it, it's the same caterpillar, only its body molecules were deeply transformed and restructured, allowing it to be quite different. We can summarize the process like this:

❖Origin: caterpillar: an animal with an inferior body
❖Process: metamorphosis: restructuring of the inferior animal's molecules (the caterpillar's)
❖Result: caterpillar with wings or butterfly: animal with a superior body, that is the result of a molecular restructuring process that turned an inferior animal into a physically superior one.

To understand who you really are, I want you to open your mind and your heart.

My grandfather used to tell me how the Universe was created. He told me that before anything existed, before the Universe existed, there was only a tremendous amount of energy, similar to the sun. There was a sphere of energy in motion but with no growth, no solid body. It was pure energy, and they called it *Hunab Ku* (the primal energy).   There were molecules that spread out like flames of fire. One day, the energy felt the wish to expand and produce new transcending forms. The first thing *Hunab Ku* did was to contract and condense all its power and strength. The energy concentration was so big that it exploded and *Nohoch Wáak´al* (big explosion) took place. Modern scientists call it the Big Bang.

During the explosion, the energy molecules of the original *Hunab Ku* became differently organized giving way to the Universe as we know it: our solar system, our planet, the water, the earth, minerals, plants, animals and, finally, it created a physical body that contained all of nature's elements in one piece. It created a very special "costume" for itself that could multiply and even transcend into higher planes or dimensions.

Hunab Ku appeared on Earth, but divided itself into two parts: *Yumm whol* (Lord Energy) and *Xuna' an whol* (Goddess Energy). In other words, *Hunab Ku* created two physical forms (men and women) with similar attributes, but at the same time, totally independent from one another. When a specimen (of each of these forms) gets together with the other one, through their sexual organs, a new *Wi' inkil whol* (energetic body or human being) is generated. This is how the original *Hunab Ku* dwells in each human being (*Wi' inkil whol*) that is born, and expands for generations without end. And you were born in one of these generations. *Hunab Ku* transformed itself into thousands of millions of human beings, each one of them being a *Wi' inkil whol* (energetic body).

In other words, your body is no more than a wrapping for *Hunab Ku* to dwell within; your essence is divine.

Today, with the diversification of languages and creeds, *Hunab Ku* is referred to in many different ways: God, Primal Force, Universal Energy, etc.

And so, just as in metamorphosis, the relationship between God and Man (*Hunab Ku* and the *Wi' inkil whol*) that I just explained can be summarized like this:

❖Origin: *Hunab Ku*: Great Universal Energy, source of all other existing energies; God.

❖Process: *Nohoch Wáak'al*, Big Bang, concentration of the total energy in a small core, where God reorganized its molecules,

❖Result: *Yumm whol* (Lord Energy) and *Xuna' an whol* (Goddess Energy). *Wi' inkil whol* (energetic body). The human being is the special "costume" used by God in the three dimensional plane, to multiply itself and transcend into other frequencies and universes.

We can look at it as follows:

The Night of the Last Katún 2012 Maya

	BUTTERFLY	HUNAB KU (GOD)
ORIGIN	Caterpillar	*Hunab Ku* (God)
PROCESS	Metamorphosis - transformation (molecule re structuring)	*Nohoch Wáak'al* – Big Bang (molecule re structuring)
RESULT	Caterpillar with wings (butterfly)	*Wi' inkil whol* (Human Being)

In short, God's molecules transformed themselves and became your body. Thus, all human beings are the "costume" God uses to participate in this dimension.

That very moment I heard *In la' ak a la akech*, buzzing in my ears. It's a Mayan phrase that means: "I am you; you are me". It was my ancestors reminding me of their philosophy.

In conclusion, the point is to understand that God lives in you as He lives in me. In Maya: *Sucum yumm cu cuxtal in tech yetel ten*, as well as in all living things.

When I saw *Yemeno' ob te kin' o* (the Descending God), engraved on Tulum's pyramid, I realized that we are all connected with *Hunab Ku*, and I understood why most archeologists arrived at the conclusion that the Maya had many gods. This is not what our ancestors said; they wanted to tell us that *Hunab Ku* is everything, under different forms and frequencies. In that sense, the whole Universe is like a huge machine where we all participate and are responsible for its correct and synchronized functioning.

To summarize, the metamorphosis process helped me grasp what our origin was and why *Hunab Ku* does not exist the way people conceive it. I finally understood why it is said that we are the temple of God, and God dwells in us and is everywhere, and I understood why the ancient Maya said we are all one, "I am you and you are me".

I wish to emphasize the most important part of my ancestors' message here. I'm not alluding to a given religion or philosophy, but it is thanks to this message that we can understand that unity is possible even when we practice different religions or follow different philosophies.

 I repeat: everything is related to everything else ...everything is part of everything else.... everything is part of *Hunab Ku*. Everything is a fragment of the Universe and is part of us humans living on this planet. We came here to experience love and unity with the totality. All humans are connected to the universal energy, and must ask themselves what they intend to do with their lives when they finish reading this book. We should all work for peace to reach the unity of mankind and, most of all, for us to reach the unity of all Mexicans (Mayas, Mexicas and Aztlans).

The big challenge here is for each person to believe he or she is part of *Hunab Ku* and is *Hunab Ku* itself, and is simultaneously part of the one consciousness. Imagine what could be done if everyone knew they were *Hunab Ku*, how far mankind could go. The possibilities are endless.

That is why *Hunab Ku* decided to grant free will to the *Wi' inkil whol* (Human Being). Remember *Hunab Ku* wears a costume, and that costume is you. We now know *Hunab Ku* has a physical body that It uses to multiply itself, but apart from multiplying itself, why does It want a physical body?, what is the function of this suit in the form of *Yumm whol* (Lord Energy) and *Xuna' an whol* (Goddess Energy)?

I was about to discover the answer to my question when the noise of some people visiting the pyramids took me out of my vision. I realized it was late afternoon; I had been meditating almost all day to gain clarity as to this message of light.

2.Antal hunab ku
(Meditation to connect yourself to your origin)

EXERCISE

My ancestors gave me the following visualization exercise to help us reconnect ourselves to our origin, and thus allow Hunab Ku –the source of all energy- to flow through our body, enabling us to develop our full potential. I have named this exercise the "potter", because it is a metaphorical way to create a neuron structure to gain understanding and become connected to our origin, in a natural way.

Tonala in Jalisco state is famous for its potters –the most famous ones in the country. They use the well known "blown glass" technique. It's very simple: they pick a piece of glass and heat it in an oven until it becomes sticky, they secure it on the extreme end of a long tube. They blow into the tube and the red-hot glass on the end is thus molded into the desired shape. This is exactly the technique we are going to use to connect ourselves to our origin. You don't need to relax just use your creativity. Closing your eyes may help you visualize better. You don't have to close your eyes, but it can help.

You will visualize three elements: First, the largest and most powerful source of energy you can imagine, with all the attributes you wish or believe. You may give it the name you wish: supreme energy, God, Hunab Ku, etc., the name doesn't matter, only the characteristics of this source of energy. Second: imagine there is an old powerful sage in this energy source. You cannot see him but you know he's there. He has a large glass tube coming out of the source that can reach out any distance. Third, imagine your body is a piece of glass of your favorite color.

Now that your brain has processed these images, you will create the following film in your mind: out of this powerful source of energy comes a long, flexible, transparent glass tube that grows longer until it reaches the Earth, and there, it finds the piece of glass: your body. Once the

The Night of the Last Katún 2012 Maya

tube is connected to your body –a formless piece of glass-, it picks it up and puts it in an oven and heats it. Then your body –this piece of glass- starts changing color. First, it becomes red and as it gets hotter it turns orange and, finally, when it has reached its hottest temperature it turns white, melting into a sticky paste. When it turns white it eliminates all the impurities in it (the glass impurities will represent here all the guilt and fears you've suffered in life). When you body has become a glowing, white, sticky glass paste, you will imagine the old sage -who lives in the source of power-blowing and blowing through the tube, creating what your body will look like. So let your imagination fly, until your body has taken the shape you chose.

Your body has now taken on the form you created. Imagine that the energy flowing down the transparent glass tube, held by the old sage, living in the power-source, is reaching into your body. Observe that as the power goes into your body it makes it shine very brightly, and you become a light power station. Your whole body glimmers and you turn everything you touch into light.

It is crucial for you to maintain a mental connection to the source of energy and power, whatever you do and wherever you are. The connection will always be available to you throughout your life, and whenever you need strength, protection or anything else, you can activate the flow of energy through the tube down to your body. The great challenge here is to remain connected to the source as long as possible.

*The energy that flows continuously down to your body can be used to heal yourself or others, to recharge your "batteries", protect yourself, become energized, etc. You decide. Remember you are whole and part of the whole at the same time. [The power-source connected to you, **IS YOU!**]*

IV SECOND MESSAGE OF LIGHT

The Night of the Last Katún 2012 Maya

1. Meyaho' ob ton pixan
(We are creators our own spirit)

I was sitting at the boarding gate in Merida's airport, waiting for my flight to Mexico City -where I was to visit the National Anthropology and History Museum- I was observing the people doing ordinary things: talking on the phone, checking their agendas or simply waiting for their flight to be announced. I noticed that as people started down the ramp into the airplane, their attitude changed. They became very serious as they sat down.. Take off was announced. People became even more tense when they felt the counter-gravity effect. The tension was tangible, you could almost touch their thoughts. I'm sure most of them were thinking of God, or else, about life and death. Has this ever happened to you?

Later on, when we experienced turbulence, a similar restlessness was felt. Finally, the last stressful moments were felt as the airplane came in for landing. It's strange how these moments make people so aware of their physical life.

When I arrived in Mexico City, I checked into a hotel and took a rest. Then I went out to begin my research –and satisfy my curiosity- as to why *Hunab Ku* had taken on human form –Its human costume-, for what purpose? We already know It used it to multiply itself but I somehow intuited this was not its main purpose.

I took a tour of the National Anthropology and History Museum to admire what was there and to try to find the key to interpret the ancient messages. I visited several halls, and observed many archeological pieces loaded with information. After my tour, I went out to take a stroll to clear my thoughts.

As I was walking in the Chapultepec's gardens, I became tired and sat a while to meditate. When I was deep in meditation, the music of a group of indigenous dancers came to my ear. They must have been performing a ceremony, I thought, because of the smell of incense and

The Night of the Last Katún 2012 Maya

copal (Mexican incense). They use copal incense as a purification offering and as a vehicle to contact their ancestors.

When my body was at peace, soothed and concentrated, I could visualize the group of dancers, their movements, their clothing, and their offerings. The focus of my visualization was on the *huehuetl* (a drum used in special ceremonies). Its sounds made my body cells vibrate. I could feel it like a rush of electromagnetic impulses going through my body. I then remembered that just a while ago I had seen Tenango's *huehuetl* (drum) in the museum. The beautiful engravings on its base included an eagle and a vulture or condor with extended wings. As the *huehuetl's* vibrations became more intense and harmonious, the eagle and the condor came to life and took flight. They flew in circles over me, then, went in opposite directions. The eagle flew North and the condor, South.

When I finished admiring the birds' flight, my attention came back to the *huehuetl*; its sound was more intense, and instead of the eagle and condor on its base, two other figures that I'd seen in the museum, had taken their place. One was from the Teotihuacan exhibit, the other one from the Maya exhibit.

Coming from the Teotihuacan archeological site, was the engraving of a skull inside a circle -with slightly open jaws, the tongue partially out-, there were lines running out of the skull like beams. The whole figure was inside a larger circle.. It was engraved in the place where the eagle used to be, at the base of the drum. In the area where the condor used to be, was now the image of a man with a serene expression, and a cylindrical ornament, about seven centimeters long and three centimeters thick hanging from his head. On top of the ornament were three empty circles that once held jade stones.. Over the head, lay a damaged pot, tilted forward. Finally, the face was partially touching some kind of rosette formed by three concentric circles. The largest circle was divided into twenty sections approximately, each one marked with notches. The middle circle overlapped the largest one, and had smaller notches and nine holes in it. The smallest circle was inside of the other two, and had only one hole in the middle. The concentric circles made contact with the back of the skull.

Every time the drum vibrated to the songs' rhythm, the sound gathered energy inside of it, and from there it sent it to the Earth. The waves spread out many kilometers, as though from a big explosion of high frequency waves that made all the things around it become synchronized and aligned. It was like putting a complex mechanism into synchrony, where all the pieces vibrate and move at the same time. The figures that had taken the place of the birds became alive and seemed to catch fire, letting out energy in the form of lines and circles, like neon objects going from the skull to the beams, from the face to the circles, where the fire took on different hues. Watching the energy movement was marvelous; it turned different shapes, forming figures, symbols, waves, etc.

The Night of the Last Katún 2012 Maya

All of a sudden, the voices from the ceremony came to me. They said:

When the drums beat

The jungle has its mystery
It will be revealed some day
The mystery is the sound
Produced by the drum

Ao Ao Ao AAooo (four times)

When the drums beat
And your heart hears the beat
Your mind remembers
your ancient life

Ao Ao Aoo AAooo (four times)

When the drums beat
The spirits come down
When they smell the incense
And the odor of *copal*

Ao Ao Ao   AAoo (four times)

I met the song's author a few months later, "grandfather" Francisco Gómez, who gives continuity to the traditions of our ancestors through the ceremonies that he organizes in Mexicali, Mexico.

I was exhilarated and blissful as I grasped the meaning of my vision and of the song I had just heard. Knowledge lay in perfect synchrony, and I had found access to it. Now everything seemed logical; the message had been there, plain to see, for many years. Why couldn't people see it?

The Night of the Last Katún 2012 Maya

When I finished my activities in Mexico City, I got in touch with a woman friend I have in the beautiful city of Puebla, in Puebla State. I arrived there early and went directly to the main square. My mind was spinning with the figures from the museum: frequencies, ultrasonic vibrations, subsonic vibrations, energy... Downtown, I bought myself a delicious, steaming cup of coffee and I sat on a bench to drink it. The morning was splendid, the sun shone brightly; lending an exquisite touch of chilliness and sunshine at the same time. The great volcano Popocatepetl lay regally, in the distance, with its snow-covered heights.

My friend arrived punctually at 9 o'clock. As an architect, she is well acquainted with ancient buildings, so we agreed to start our tour in the main square –where we met- and from there go to the main churches of the city. The special beauty of each church is impressive! As we admired them, my friend pointed out the architectural differences between one and the other. Some were similar, while others were totally different from the rest.

Puebla is an extremely beautiful city and it has a peculiar name: "Puebla de los Angeles" (Puebla of the Angels). Someone once explained this name to me. When they were building the cathedral of the city, it was quite impossible to lift the extremely large and heavy bells all the way up the main tower. So the workers decided to leave the task for the next day explaining they would lift them with special cranes. But lo and behold when they arrived there the next day, the bells were already up in their place. The angel sculptures that used to guard the entrance hall had disappeared, so people assumed that those angels were responsible for raising the bells. And that is why the city's emblem is a bell with an angel on each side.

Interestingly enough, whether legend or fact people truly believe it. And when two or more people believe something, it becomes real (because it produces a frequency). The second message of light came to my mind at that moment. When we finished our coffee, we headed to Cholula, which is just a few minutes away from Puebla.

The Night of the Last Katún 2012 Maya

By the time we arrived in the village, we were very hungry so we walked directly to the market. People in this town are very peaceful and quiet. How could they not be when they live in such a charming and traditional town? After eating a delicious dish made of grass-hoppers and *nopales* (cactus), we walked to a building that looked like an observatory. The marvels of Mexico never cease to amaze me.

I saw a large open area that had a 20 meter high (65 ft.) wooden post with a square wooden structure on top. Five indigenous people were sitting on it. Four of them were tied to the structure by their ankles; the fifth one was sitting in the center, ready to play the pre Hispanic flute. These indigenous people are known as the *Papantla* "flying dancers" (originally from Veracruz state).

The ceremony performed by the *Papantla* fliers signifies that we come "from the sun". The fliers spin head first all the way to the ground forming a spiral that reminds us that we are an inexhaustible source of energy, and become human when we come to Earth. Do you realize that regardless of the culture, the message is always the same? We come from and are part of a great source of energy.

It was a week day and there weren't many people in town, so we had a chance to relax and enjoy the fascinating sight, and even meditate a while. We sat on the church's staircase, on top of the earthen pyramid. From where I sat, I had a complete view of the surroundings: the passersby, the pyramid, the hill, the volcanoes (Popocatepetl and Iztacchihuatl), the churches, and the indigenous people in the country. Each feature contributed to this beautiful landscape, yet preserving its individual harmony and charm. Some twenty minutes had gone by when we heard the sound of the *ocarinas* (indigenous flutes), because the descent of the *Papantla* flyers had started. They came down, spinning head first, around the post.

As I watched them, I went into a meditative state and back to the thoughts I had had in Chapultepec Park. I decided to analyze the vision I had when I first heard the drum and had heard the song "When the drums beat". I understood that our thoughts are dynamic energy that produces vibration and sound. The figures engraved on the wooden base of the *drum* became extremely meaningful to me. The skull figure with beams coming out of it shone more intensively all over, as the *drum* played. It was like the sun illuminating everything around it.

What I then observed was that the sounds of the drum penetrated down to the bones of the dancers, mainly the skull, turning their skeletal structure into a resonating instrument, and making the dancers' bodies shine. In turn, the dancer's bodies retransmitted the vibrations to all of the spectators around them, raising their energy to a higher vibration.

Because of the high vibration, their brain developed new neuron connections, activating their endocrine system so that it could produce more hormones and pheromones that permeated the surroundings.

The Mayan face engraved on the other side of the drum absorbed the sound and produced different levels of frequency, that went from sonic (audible) to ultrasonic (non audible) frequencies. The lower frequencies of the people around the dancers automatically rose to a harmonious vibration, regardless of what they were thinking at that moment.

When I was dwelling upon these things, I remembered that in one of my electronics classes I had done some research on frequencies and sounds, and I recalled there were three main kinds of sounds: sonic, subsonic and ultrasonic. The sonic vibration is the one we normally hear. The subsonic vibration is transmitted at low frequencies. The ultrasonic sound is transmitted at high frequencies. All of the living dwellers of this planet are sensitive to all three frequencies, and may absorb, produce or transmit them.

So when two or more people think of the same thing, a certain vibration is produced; it can be transmitted to other people, no matter what type of vibration. I think this is crucial to our purpose of awakening people's consciousness and preparing ourselves for the great 2012 world event. Ultrasonic sound, as its name indicates, is produced by a high acoustic vibration. They have a limited range that requires broadcasting antennas to reach their destination. The human brain can produce ultrasound vibrations when the person is happy, content and they are in a state of harmony and balance. "Modern" human beings do not always reach such a vibration due to various factors. This does not mean that human beings cannot produce such a frequency but that they produce it rarely in their lifetime, and not consistently. Other things that also produce ultrasonic frequencies are: ancient ceremonies, dances, chants, burning incense and *copal,* the drum beat or the *huub* (conch shell which can produce a rather pleasant sound of ultrasonic vibration), prayer, meditation and remaining in a state of inner peace.

Subsonic frequency is produced by low frequency sounds. These sounds do not require broadcasting antennas because their vibration does not collide with any elements we find in nature. They can travel great distances, the length of a continent, before they weaken. Human beings can also produce this kind of frequency; they'll produce it when they're under stress or in a negative state of mind (envy, resentment, hatred, fear, corruption, neurosis, low self-esteem, etc.), lack of contact with nature, lack of physical caresses, lack of affection. Unfortunately, human beings produce these kinds of frequencies most of their lives.

I will give you an example of how these frequencies function in animal life (the same applies to human beings): when animals are wounded, sick or trapped, their brain emits subsonic sounds, and their endocrine system produces hormones (odors) that travel great distances together with sound. Predators capture these odors and frequencies and their guiding system may lead them towards their prey. When animals hunt, if there is a wounded or sick member of the herd, predators will perceive their subsonic frequencies and will attack those first.

Human beings produce pheromones in a similar way through their endocrine system and perceive frequencies through the brain, but most people produce subsonic vibrations (and their corresponding odors). People around them absorb them and become contaminated, reacting in the same way. Humans have more than twenty receptors in the nose and are able to perceive most of the odors in the environment. Once the brain captures them, it builds a new neuron net to continue producing and reproducing the same odors it has unconsciously absorbed.

The Night of the Last Katún 2012 Maya

Let's analyze in more detail: our neurons are energetic receptors; in other words, they are sensitive to the energetic vibrations in the environment, within a given low to high vibration range. Our brain emits vibration frequency waves, which have a certain relationship with the different states of awareness of the individual. Every time you emit micro electric impulses, although they are not visible to the eye, your head becomes literally warmer, particularly if you become obsessed with a given thought.

The deeper we go into relaxation or deep breathing, the lower brain activity or frequency we can reach. It means that if we learn to control our breath rhythm we may learn to control our brain frequency, thus, our thoughts. Remember that neurons can perceive different thought frequencies produced at that moment or that were produced before, not necessarily just in the present.

That's why our country is asleep. It's like we are submerged in a deep cloud of subsonic frequencies and odors covering the whole country, which gives existence to a system of limited and negative concepts that affect all the Mexican people. Indeed, during the conquest, an enormous vibration of subsonic frequency was produced by the murders, rape, pillage, etc. that came over the country. Such frequency was transmitted from one generation to the next, over the years (through odor) until today and no one has been able to change this. That is why the Mexican people remain in some kind of lethargic state, allowing all kinds of abuse from others. As more people are born, this frequency becomes stronger.

Because all of us are submerged in this subsonic frequency, we are not aware of it, so each human being enters in this vibration unconsciously, expanding it continuously. That is why individuals think that life is like that and there is no other way to live. But, in reality, negativity exists because we make it stronger, more powerful.

If we wish to perceive life a different way, we simply have to create the necessary consciousness. I'm going to give you an example. Computers did not exist until a few years ago. However, people today need them for most of their activities. Internet did not exist either. Today, most businesses and homes count on that service. Not to mention cell phones; they're absolutely indispensable today. You hardly see city people who don't carry a cell phone. That is what marketing is all about: first they build the need in you for something (thought frequency), then you don't even have to be pushed to go out and get it. As salesmen say "We are not selling, you are purchasing" or "We don't sell, we satisfy your needs". That's how it is; first the frequency is created and, later, you live in it and continue to walk in the same vicious cycle. If you pay attention; you'll see that all of the technology you hold so dear, did not exist a while ago, and we managed without it!

Likewise, we can create an energetic vibration where we can live in peace, harmony and love (without having to use any negative frequency). We need three things to create this: first, the need to do it; second, to create the frequency, and third, the responsibility to continue creating this frequency through practice.

We already have the first part of this process -need-. Just observe the chaos we live in. The second part about creating the frequency is explained in the sub-chapter *Ka' anal Humm* (ultrasound). The third part is up to you: all you have to do is assume responsibility of practicing and spreading the new frequency.

When I arrived in the country's capital, I clearly saw the contamination phenomenon (that I had observed on the airplane). All of the passengers were contaminated with the thoughts (vibrations) of the other passengers; they all became attuned to the same fearful mood or frequency. The same thing happened when I arrived in Mexico City. Most people were influenced by the newspapers, magazines and media in general, they were attuned to a subsonic frequency of fear, pain, sickness, robbery, violence, abduction, etc. Because the majority of people were thinking of those things, the minority of people who tried to maintain positive thinking ended up feeling exhausted, and were later overwhelmed by the low frequency thoughts. Nobody ever taught them how to control their thoughts. We tend to think too much, which takes much of our energy and stirs our low frequency emotions, such as: jealousy, envy, resentment, hatred, etc.

I concluded that each *Wi' inkil whol* (human being) is responsible for creating their own concepts, beliefs and paradigms. In short, each individual is responsible for their own vibrations, and at the same time, each one decides which vibration (subsonic or ultrasonic) they shall transmit.

The courses, talks, lectures, seminars and workshops that I've imparted have been attended by people of different religions, social class, political affiliations, and creeds. But, who are these people? Why did they come? I stopped to think about this and came to the conclusion that they are people who pursue change, who are seeking for progress, who were sick and tired of living the same life and pursuit of happiness, people who thought they could undergo a radically change some day.

The questions that came to my mind were: Why do we seek happiness? What is happiness in itself? What is it made of? And what does happiness have to do with vibration, sound, frequency? That moment I was able to reach a clear understanding of why *Hunab Ku* had created the *Wi' inkil whol* endowing it at the same time with free will. The second message of light became crystal clear to me.

Our physical body is in itself the expansion and transcendence of *Hunab Ku*. He created an energetic body (human being) for itself and endowed it with a nervous system, an endocrine system, a respiratory system, the capacity to smell, and a neuron structure that would be able to "perceive" and "create" a spiritual body.

Every time you think and activate emotions or feelings, you are creating an energetic cell with a spiritual frequency. I will explain: your physical body is made of millions of cells, forming your organs, skin, hair, and all of your body. As you grow, more and more cells are produced every day, with the food you eat.

Likewise -on a spiritual level- every time your brain is activated and produces a thought, your emotions and feelings are activated, and a new spiritual cell is generated. This is what the thought process is all about. As you grow up and generate thoughts, your spiritual body grows too, just like your physical body. Every human being living on the planet is, thus, responsible for creating their own spiritual body.

In other words, your spiritual body is formed by your thoughts, beliefs, concepts and ideas. They accumulate in your spiritual body and every time you need them, your brain becomes active and contacts your spiritual body and downloads what it needs, in the form of memory. Remember, for instance, what you just did a few minutes ago. You can remember it because it is a spiritual cell. No matter when you recall it, the spiritual cell is with you, because you've created it, and it will be there forever. No matter what you think, no matter what you've experienced, whether good or bad, every time you activate your brain, your emotions and feelings will create a spiritual cell. In this fashion you create you spiritual body, and this energetic body remains there forever, because when your physical body ceases to exist, your spiritual body (spiritual cells) transcends intact to other frequencies. And I hope it can, because for you to leave this plane, an substantial amount of high frequency (ultrasonic) energy is needed.

Hunab Ku was very intelligent; It created a physical body to grow and expand and, thus, transport its energy to other frequencies. And It does it through every human being. That is why It gave you the complex body you have. So all of the resources you need to expand through happiness are already in you. God gave you an emotional life to expand your love and joy, to evolve and develop all the positive aspects you wish to expand. However, ignorance may take you in the opposite direction, to the point where you may be here without even knowing that you came to this world to build a high frequency spiritual body. You may be devoting your precious time merely to survive, and in doing so you accumulate hatred, jealousy, a manipulative attitude, resentment, neurosis, bitterness, etc. You use the complexity of your body to go in the wrong direction. That is why it gave you free will. Now that you know why you came to this planet, it is up to you to either continue on the path of ignorance, pursuing goals that bring you no true happiness, or to change the course of your life and follow a path that will lead you to spiritual growth.

Whether God will expand and transcend through your actions and thinking is up to you; this is free will. When you reach this understanding, you can grow and raise your energetic vibration.

Now that you know your spiritual body is made of your thoughts, what are you going to do? I've told you that every time you think, you activate emotions and feelings, and this generates new cells in your spiritual body. Your brain sees no good or bad; it only processes your thoughts and generates spiritual cells. So you produce your own spiritual body through the experiences you create for yourself day after day, every second of your life. That is why it is so important that you be happy and joyful.

Your body was built to create experiences, and every experience is a new cell in your spiritual body. This is the way *Hunab Ku* grows and expands its energetic body. So you are responsible for making your spiritual body grow and making *Hunab Ku's* energetic body expand, at the same time. That is why you were endowed with emotions and feelings, so you can generate an extraordinary kind of energy every day that will make you feel the extraordinary being that you are.

Your purpose or mission on Earth is to produce experiences that will make you happy. No one is responsible for your mission except you. If you feel low frequency emotions like jealousy, envy, resentment, depression, it is because you haven't unraveled the true meaning of life; you are waiting for others to come and make you happy; you are waiting for others to bring you the joy you need... but it is not their responsibility; it is **YOURS!**

You were born unlabeled into this world. Nobody has a manual to tell you how to be happy or how to behave. It's up to you to decide. The only rule is not to hurt others and to be clear as to what you want. No one has a right to judge you because they don't know what is imprinted on your spiritual body. And no one can tell you what you must imprint on your spiritual body. This only concerns you.

Your mission upon arrival to this plane is to produce ultrasonic energy, which is the frequency you generate when you are happy, joyous, when you're doing the things you like. It's the only way you can make *Hunab Ku* evolve. If you're not happy, and instead you're constantly in pain, sick, and letting off low frequencies, you are generating subsonic energy which keeps you from evolving both physically and spiritually.

You are mature enough to follow your own judgment; you can understand that everyone has a right to be different and experience life in their own way. When you reach this understanding you have reached a level of acceptance. But what prevents you from accepting people as they are? The mental structures in your brain since childhood, because most people are taught competition and power at an early age. Your family unconsciously tells you that you must be the best in your class, and be on the honor roll, in short, they teach you to compete with others.

They also teach you the power structure. You perceive men as more powerful than women, as in the animal kingdom, which leads to a macho culture. A classic example is when you do something wrong, and your mother threatens you: "you'll see when your father comes home!" We grew up in a society where women have an inferior position in comparison to the men in the family. Rarely, does the *xtub* (the youngest child) contribute an opinion or an idea that is different from the accustomed values. This is what leads to family conflict.

Spirituality is a synonym of happiness. Happiness is the measure of your spiritual growth. Some people know a lot about spirituality but don't put it into practice. They are knowledgeable individuals but not truly spiritual. Spirituality does not only have to do with religion, but it is based on diversity. Each one has a growing rhythm. Each one has their own understanding of life. Just enjoy what you personally practice. Evolution occurs thanks to diversity.

If we analyze our life carefully –particularly our beliefs and mental structures- we'll see that the idea of competition was instilled in us early in life. Our whole educational system is based on competition more than sharing. This doesn't mean that competing is not good; it just doesn't apply in every area of our life and, least of all, in spirituality.

Hunab Ku does not compete with anyone; It truly wants unity. What does It want unity for? For the sake of progress, naturally. No one, listen to me, and I write this in capital letters, **NO ONE, ABSOLUTELY NO ONE** can compete on a spiritual level. Spirituality is an interior experience, something you enjoy inside. No religion is better than another, no ceremony is better than another. The true power rests in accepting and sharing with others, for the sake of unity. There is no religion, creed or philosophy that could separate us; what is really separating us is our ego, and our competitive frame of mind.

When there is ego without spirituality, things become inharmonious and imbalanced because they become confrontational. Even evolution becomes slower because, before anything else, you must struggle against the ego of the people in power and in control. For example, if you're working in an enterprise, and your boss has ego but no spirituality, you must fight against his ego before you can make your voice come forward. If you know how to do some things, your direct boss would surely block your ideas from reaching the general director. When there is ego but spirituality as well, you think not only about yourself but about the group and about the benefit of all including yourself, because spirituality (joy) elevates your frequency to a point where you want to share it with others. Remember what happens when you're blissful: you want others to participate in your bliss; better ideas come to you and you even accept other people's ideas, because your ego is sharing a group mentality. And even when ego is completely individualistic, you feel proud of contributing your ideas, and doing things for others. Every thing changes, everything is different, everything is better.

The Maya have left you a clear message in this respect. Go to Palenque and you will find there remains of a diversified culture, from their architecture to their lifestyle. There is no place for "spiritual competition", but rather for "spiritual sharing", where everybody feels respect for others and they accept each other and live in peace and harmony, sharing a super consciousness based on unity and diversification. They knew there would be competition and power conflicts derived from "ego-ridden spirituality".   In the absence of spirituality, ego comes to the surface. Ego is not always a bad thing if you can use it with spirituality. If you use ego with no spirituality you'll cause damage to others and to yourself, but if you are a truly spiritual person, you can use ego without harming anyone.

Finally, I understood why the leaders: *Ahau Tah, Ahau Itzá and Ahau Pakal* proclaimed themselves as *Kukulk'an Quetzalcoatl* (as God, Allah, Supreme Power, Universal Energy).These Mayan spiritual guides proclaimed themselves as *Kukulk'an Quetzalcoatl* because they had reached spiritual awakening or, in modern terms, they had become illuminated. I came to understand why my grandparents had told me that there would be many people on my path who would try to make me believe in *Hunab Ku*. They warned me to never believe only in *Hunab Ku*, because this mistake has led the world to chaos.

When I think of this piece of advice my grandparents gave me, I realize that they were right: believing in God is not the same as feeling part of Him. Most people only believe in *Hunab Ku*. Believing in Him is simple and irresponsible because that way you don't have to assume any responsibility. You can do as you please, and you know He's going to forgive you because He is a loving father. You can prove this idea by conducting a simple survey. Ask people in jail if they believe in *Hunab Ku*; ask those who mistreat their children, those who contaminate the rivers, the oceans, ask the jealous, the neurotic, the depressive, ask those who hurt their peers. They will tell you that they certainly believe in *Hunab Ku*. It's easy to leave one's responsibility to Him. It's easy to shun one's responsibility to love, to accept, to forgive, and to promote the harmony and balance of the planet we live in.

The negativity in our lives has been passed down to us since the conquest, when the people that arrived in our country killed us, robbed us, raped us in the name of God. Today 500 years later, our people are still asleep and haven't overcome such a negative heritage. However, things can change when you feel part of God, and assume your responsibility in preserving the planet in perfect balance. You must not contaminate the planet or hurt it, nor hurt anyone; you must be attuned with your peers. You must see people as they are, and let them be themselves without your interference. You have no right to possess anyone with your jealousy. You cannot hurt them or stop them from having their own experiences. Also, you must not cause any damage to your body. You must not feel depressed. If you feel depressed, it's because you feel trapped in a society whose beliefs limit your personal expression. You must always do right; do the things that lead to harmony and balance. Do you see the difference between "believing and being"?

The majority of people who've tried to interpret the knowledge that our ancestors left us have been mistaken. Most people thought that the *Maa yab* people were polytheist who worshiped many gods: the god of water, of wind, of fire, of earth, of rain, of the sun, etc..They believed we practiced sacrifices to appease our god's rage. But the true message is that everything is part of ourselves, everything is connected; though on different frequencies, everything is one and the same. Everything comes from the same primal energy *Hunab Ku*, and it is our responsibility to respect and be in balance with our own essence, because we are part of the whole, nothing is separate from us. Our ancestors couldn't have left us contradictory messages: those that assert we come from *Hunab Ku* , and those that promote worshiping the elements. We must apply reason to things we read or hear. History has been manipulated and changed to a point where much of what is said does not correspond to the truth.

It is your responsibility to exercise free will and think deeply on what is written here.

After *Hunab Ku* transformed itself into thousands of millions of gods (human beings), his idea was to form unity, and that is why he gave us free will. This is our big challenge as *Yumm whol* and *Xuna' an whol* (gods-goddesses, energetic beings): to become united, share with others and accept ourselves as we are; to know that in spite of our differences we can live together and form the universal body of *Hunab Ku*. Only when we reach this level of consciousness will we be able to evolve and bring peace and harmony into the world.

No one has tried this before; let's get together today for the same purpose: reaching peace, sharing with others and accepting them, regardless of religion, creed, philosophy, social class, political affiliations, sex or age. It's our opportunity to awaken as the children of the new sun, as it was prophesied by the *Maa yab*.

You did not create me and make me come to planet Earth simply to survive and pass the time. You brought me here to remember who You are, and to ensure the awakening of consciousness, and to show the people that unity is possible, and that we are all *Hunab ku* and part of It at the same time, and to show the people that only together will we evolve towards a better world. But this is our decision –I remind you-; the world has split in two: those who cause damage and those who try to heal the planet. By exercising your free will, through action, the balance will shift towards the side you take.

The sun was setting when my friend called and told me "I saw you were deep in your thoughts and I did not want to interrupt you, because I thought it was something important, but you haven't eaten anything since breakfast." So we started down the hill leaving the pyramid behind. I felt happy and content with the reflections I'd had. As we hiked down hill, we talked and I told her part of the visualization I'd had. Because she's an architect, she was able to understand more clearly the purpose of the ancient buildings, why they were built facing a certain direction, were made of certain materials and, most of all, why they had a given shape. For example, when you walk into an ancient cathedral in our country, you feel a different vibration at once, because those kinds of constructions generate frequencies that you can almost touch. Those places can sometimes generate ultrasonic frequencies, others can generate subsonic frequencies, especially in places where torture, physical pain and murder were practiced by the Inquisition.

An idea that also came to my mind was that while our brain is wired so it can generate subsonic frequencies (suffering, victimization complex, etc.), we become addicted to those kinds of energies. We become addicted to a low frequency kind of life, and so we seek for painful circumstances that will cause pain, grief, difficulties. Therefore, we must change such structures in order to generate ultrasonic frequencies that will transform us into luminous beings. We must activate the genetic codes in us that will lead us to a higher understanding of who we really are, but most of all, to change the circumstances of our life. This is so, because we are reaching a time when the Earth shall vibrate at ultrasonic frequencies, through the beam that will raise its frequency. We must align ourselves to this frequency.

You must realize that day after day, the Earth is increasing its frequency, and humans are starting to vibrate at these higher frequencies. That is why more people are being affected by bipolarity or schizophrenia. There are greater numbers of people who experience such perceptions. They have been currently diagnosed as mentally ill, but they are in fact developing new abilities that they must learn to control, otherwise humans won't be able to fit in this new vibration.

The subsonic frequency world (fear) is about to disappear, but you must be very careful because its emitting its last low frequencies: new sicknesses based on fear appear every day, like the HINI influenza; more people come down with cancer every day, but this is nothing more than the manifestation of the low vibrations that we are generating.

As my friend and I came down from the pyramid, two new doubts came to me: if my ancestors were capable of handling frequencies, sounds, vibrations, what did they do to make a person generate ultrasound? How did they transmit ultrasound frequencies among themselves? That very moment, I received a message on my cell phone that resolved my doubt.

The Night of the Last Katún 2012 Maya

2. Het'dz a tu' ukul

(Dynamics to control your thinking)

Throughout the years, I've tried different meditation methods to control thought, until I found the simplest one. I found out that when you use it, your thoughts literally come to a halt, providing you with the opportunity to choose the reflection you want, in order to process the appropriate emotion. It seems far fetched, but this is how thinking actually works: first you choose a thought and then your body "automatically" develops the corresponding emotion.

You don't need to go into deep relaxation or to assume a certain body posture; all you need to do is use your imagination. You take a piece of paper or an object that you usually use: a wallet, a watch, etc., something small preferably. You take it in your hand and place it in front of you. Now with your imagination, you are going to draw eyes on this object and you will pretend it's looking at you. Now move your hand to one side, to the other, up, down, everywhere –you don't have to look at the object-, just imagine it is looking at you from wherever you place it. That's all you have to do. Isn't it simple? Now you will ask yourself how a simple method can yield results and stop your thinking.

I'm inviting you to try and use these dynamics for several days, and convince yourself of the results you can reach with them. I resort to this method all the time to control my thoughts and emotions. Don't play victim anymore and take responsibility for your thoughts; after all, you decide how you wish to interpret the situations and circumstances that you face every day.

3. Tsikbal
(A metaphor to analyze)

One day, a person was walking towards a town, but before going in, he decided to rest under a big tree. At that moment, he noticed a cemetery right in front of him.

He felt curious to visit the cemetery. When he came closer, he discovered that all of the graves had children in them. The gravestones had inscriptions like; Mary 5 years old, Peter 7 years old, Joanne 3 years old and so on. So this person thought an epidemic had struck the town killing many of its children.

When he saw someone nearby, he went over and asked him what had happened, why so many children had died, and if there had been an epidemic in town.

The local replied there had not been any epidemic, and those in the graves were not exactly children. Then he explained they had a tradition in that town: when a person was born, their relatives prepared a book with blank pages to register in it the happy moments this person would have throughout their life. So every time the person had a good experience, they would write it down in the book, specifying how long this happy moment had lasted, and so on.

When the person died, their children would take out the book and add the happy moments their father or mother had had. They took the sum total of such moments as the person's spiritual age.

Dear reader, if you could count and add up all the happy moments of your life, would your spiritual body have the same age as your physical body? I suggest you reflect upon this metaphor so you begin to generate more highly spiritual (happy) experiences.

I am not familiar with the author of this metaphor, but whoever it is must be someone with a very high spiritual consciousness.

V. THIRD MESSAGE OF LIGHT

The Night of the Last Katún 2012 Maya

1. Tuunich Quetzal
Kíin (Maa yab
technology)

The message I received on the cell phone was from my daughter and it said: "If you clap in front of a pyramid, it makes the sound of a *quetzal.*"
"Belló, belló! ('That's it!, that's it!', as we say in Maya)"
At that very moment I was able to test my daughter's assertion; When I clapped at the staircase of the Cholula pyramids it was just like she said (they sounded like the *Chichen Itzá* pyramids in Yucatan, like the Teotihuacán pyramids in the state of Mexico, and like many others, as I found out later) I felt elated because I had discovered it is possible to awaken our consciousness and take the quantum leap that scientists had mentioned and our ancestors had prophesied. My daughter provided me with the clue to decipher the third message of light that her king had given her.

The true functioning of our brain became clear to me; it is perfectly valid to compare it with certain electric devices like television, radio and cell phones. Their functioning is based on frequencies; their chips are the equivalent of our neurons transmitting or receiving energy frequencies.

Before I share my discovery with you, let me tell you about the "*quetzal* bird". It lives in the Mayan jungle, mainly between Chiapas and Guatemala. Its color is of an astonishing green; its tail's feathers can reach more than a meter (39 inches) long. The Maya considered this bird a symbol of freedom because when free, its plumage is exotic and spectacularly bright, but when it's captive, its feathers wither and become opaque. After some time, the bird plucks its feathers and even causes itself a heart attack because it cannot withstand captivity. And that is why the Maya took the *quetzal* as a symbol of their culture: a free civilization!

After visiting *Cholula* we had lunch. Then I went to the hotel to rest and dwell upon the information I had received. Once in my room I felt like sleeping to recover from the long trip and the day's activities. I fell fast asleep and in my sleep I had a vision.

I saw the *Chichen Itzá* pyramid; around it were many people singing, clapping and playing instruments. First, a group of thirteen people arrived, who were like guides of the different areas of the Mayan territory.   Each individual was carrying a *huub* (conch) nicely ornamented with stones of different colors. When they played this ancestral musical instrument, the pyramid produced a vibration, letting off sound frequencies. Then the *Maa Yab* territory lit up like a huge source of neon light.

Then, more guides arrived totaling a 130. Each group was dressed differently, but they all carried their *conch*. They came from far away lands in different attires, but carrying the same kind of *conch*. They all gathered around the pyramid blowing their *conches* to produce sound, then the entire American continent lit up with the same kind of light just as the *Maa yab* territory had. At the end came the most spectacular part of my vision: I saw our galaxy, a multicolor beam coming out of its center. The beam made our sun produce a huge flame that expanded all through the galaxy. The flame did not burn but carried a tremendous amount of energy, and the flame let off ultrasonic frequencies that covered the Earth.   On top of the *Chichen Itzá* pyramid were four *Kukulk'an Quetzalcoatls* meditating in the lotto position, facing each *Baakab* (cardinal direction)..

As the pyramid absorbed the ultrasonic vibration of the sun, one thousand and three hundred spiritual leaders from different nations arrived, all carrying a conch. They all gathered around the pyramid and made their *conches* sound; the sound and vibration was awesome. Then I saw the *Chichen Itzá* pyramid vibrate and transmit the ultrasonic frequencies coming from the *Bajun huubo' ob huub*" (many conches) and the sound coming from the sun. These vibrations reverberated in all the pyramids of the country; then the pyramids sent them out in all directions through the oceans: the Gulf of Mexico, the Pacific Ocean and the Caribbean Sea that surround the country.

The Night of the Last Katún 2012 Maya

The sound traveled through the waters and to outer space. In that moment, *L'amat* (Venus) worked as a satellite and sound transmitter, projecting the vibration back to the Earth again. The pyramids of Egypt, the tops of which are pointed, absorbed the vibrations and dispersed them around them, and at the same time, they retransmitted them to the Earth's interior.

Egypt is full of deserts and it doesn't have many obstacles that could stop the frequency waves from running free. The winds took the frequency waves all the way to India where its crested temples (hollow shapes on the top of buildings like the ones in *Palenque*, Chiapas state in Mexico) absorbed the vibrations, retransmitting them to their whole territory.

China also received ultrasonic frequencies through its pagodas, which in turn retransmitted them to other parts of their territory; there were pagodas all over China, just like pyramids in Mexico.

Finally, I observed the whole planet become silent and dark for three days, and on the third day the Earth lit up with a kind of light that did not blind the eye, and the energy one could feel at that moment was harmonious, and made people go into a trance or ecstasy.

What I saw in my vision was awesome. To my good luck, it lasted long because I fell sound asleep and did not wake up until next day. Then, as soon as I woke up I buckled down to write my vision for I knew it was part of the messages of light my ancestors were giving me.

The pyramids work as energy broadcasters or ultrasound frequency transmitters, like a radio station. I will explain my vision in detail. People around the pyramid were thirteen, and they were playing thirteen conchs. For the Maya, thirteen is the highest brain vibration, that is 13 hertz. It is also the vibration the Earth will reach in 2012 when the cosmic cross is formed (planetary alignment between Mars, Uranus, Saturn, the Moon, and the Earth in the center). Also, thirteen hertz is the sound produced by solar flames. Thirteen hertz are ultrasound and we produce them whenever we feel happy and blissful.

The main pyramid of *Chichen Itzá* began to vibrate and send out ultrasound waves that traveled hundreds of kilometers until they hit another pyramid which in turn worked as a broadcasting antenna sending its signal to other pyramids and so forth until the whole globe was covered.   Then the number of people playing their conches increased from 13 to 130, then to 1,300.   The number of hertz was constant but the power increased making the Earth become totally lit.

That is why the pyramids of Mexico, the Egyptian pyramids, the gongs and pagodas of the Chinese dynasties, and the sacred temples of India, are magnetically aligned and built strategically to produce, reproduce and transmit ultrasound.

Pyramids are a natural technology, built by our ancestors to transmit ultrasound frequencies that activate the pineal gland of the brain, opening up perception to a wider range of spiritual frequencies and, thus, for us to become aware that we are part of a whole. It also triggers an energetic reaction in our body that awakens dormant DNA information, to reach an awakening and expansion of consciousness.

At the beginning of time, we had 64 active DNA codes, but when the Earth entered it sleep stage, human beings stopped producing ultrasound (happiness, joy) and therefore the body also went into a stage of unawareness. Therefore, of the 64 DNA codes, only 20 are active today. The remaining 42 are activated every time we produce ultrasonic frequencies in a regular fashion. In other words, if we remained happy, joyful and blissful most of our lifetime, these codes would become naturally active.

This is the moment to generate ultrasonic frequencies.

The Mayan messages are telling us that an era of light is coming   where we can all evolve towards a high spiritual frequency, without negativity, if everyone assumes their responsibility. The moment has arrived to do something; the moment of awakening our awareness has arrived, just

The Night of the Last Katún 2012 Maya

like the ancient sages – *the Maa yab* people- envisioned.

The Yucatan pyramids –mainly the *Chichen Itzá* pyramid, probably the oldest on the continent, and the only one that survived almost intact- are ready to receive and retransmit the ultrasonic frequencies of the Universe. *Chichen Itzá* is the main energetic center that will activate the energy that we will receive from the planetary alignment, but most of all, from the solar explosions that are taking place more frequently all the time. Every time the internal explosions of the sun produce large flares, it sends a great amount of heat to the Earth, at the same time the heat lets off ultrasounds that promote the awakening of consciousness in human beings, and it does so by activating their DNA genetic codes. Keep this in mind!

Most pyramids that were destroyed and pillaged lost their original energetic value. However, even at their lowest vibration capacity, they continue to retransmit frequencies that help to raise human consciousness. But most important is the information they provide us in relation to our ancestors' technology and how they used it.

The pyramids' message transmitting function put my brain to work so I too could become a transmitter of information, but using modern tools that could cover all Mexico and even reach beyond our borders, in order to create the new frequency of the super consciousness. I shall explain this later.

That is why my daughter told me that the clapping sound bouncing on the pyramids' walls sounded like the *quetzal*. As a logical conclusion, if the sound of the pyramids is similar to the *quetzal*'s song, it means that this sound or frequency makes people reach freedom consciousness. Therefore, the chanting and clapping in my dream were messages of very high spiritual vibration, they were thoughts of light and love that could lead humans to freedom.

These visions solved the doubts I had when I was in Cholula. My doubts were solved but I also realized the enormous responsibility that this implied for me. But I felt confident and I knew I could do it. How? I did not know, but I felt ready to do whatever it took to reactivate the ultrasonic frequencies; so I decided to remain in a receptive state all of the time.

During the trips that followed, as I came into contact with more awakened beings, I developed a strategy that would enable us to transmit the frequencies that would help us activate our DNA,.

VI. WHAT TO DO WITH THE PUZZLE

The Night of the Last Katún 2012 Maya

1. Le Balo' Bo Chuc' Pa-ha' n
(What to do with the puzzle)

After several years of traveling in search of the pieces that completed the puzzle, I went back to Merida city to dwell upon the messages of light to be more prepared to transmit them later.

Between 2005 and 2006, my ancestors asked me to go and wake up and unite the ancient cultures to create a frequency that would keep my energy in balance, and to be prepared to face the events of *Hunab Ku* (moon eclipse: last cosmic event of the last *katún*). I was also instructed to cleanse and purify my country's atmosphere as part of the preparation for the changes to come.

So I began a long journey with three friends. Jorge, an inseparable friend whom I'd met in secondary school, was one of them. We visited the states of Campeche, Veracruz, Puebla, Morelos, Oaxaca, Guanajuato, to awaken the spiritual world through meditation and the *ocarina* music (kind of ancestral whistle that produces ultrasounds). We made the trip in a Chevy; it was long and adventurous. We went through all kinds of experiences; it was crazy. When we came back from the trip I continued my spiritual work, advising people on how to find their own path.

In the same year 2006, I received instructions to go to a city near the ocean, whose people were from *Aztlan* descent. As a sign they gave me, its name should include the syllable *tl*. At first, it was difficult for me to understand this revelation in depth. Around that time, I met someone who invited me to Mazatlan. I soon realized that the energy was concentrating in that city for me to continue my mission there. So I financed the trip for myself and two friends to begin my purification activity. We arrived in Mazatlan in May that year.

My ancestors told me I had to start a movement in that city, because it was the root site of our culture. Also, the most highly prepared spiritual people lived there, although they had lost track along the way, but the essence of spirituality remained alive in their descendants. All I needed was to gather thirteen individuals to generate the frequency of the super consciousness based on unity, to awaken the Mexican people.

The first time I set foot in Mazatlan, I felt blissful because I was making progress in my mission. The first thing I did was to take a rest after the long trip. I did not travel by plane; traveling on land was required to make the energy flow in that direction.

My friends were already waiting for me in Mazatlan. The next day in the morning we had coffee on the sea shore. After admiring the city's boardwalk, an unusual thought came to my mind when I was sitting on a corner at Sánchez Taboada plaza: "I'm now sitting in this place; where are the people that I am to meet?, what will they look like?"
I felt curious. I knew I was to meet many people, but very few would understand my message; most of them were still trapped in their emotions, ego, competition, the daily rhythm of modern life. I knew that the work ahead of me was not going to be easy, and even the people that were now at my side would fall back into a different vibration frequency. But my mission was to begin something in Mazatlan, and so I did.

By that time, my friends had already made arrangements for me to give a talk in a hotel auditorium. It was during that lecture that I met the person that would clear my way so I could gather enough energy to help build the new consciousness.

It was a very sunny and hot afternoon (very common in Mazatlan). The lecture had been promoted through the radio and fliers, and I had high hopes that a lot of people would show up. We had all the equipment ready: the audio, the video, so everything would go smoothly during the lecture. The event –scheduled for 6 pm- started with few participants, but among them was the woman I had to contact.

At the end of the lecture, I talked with this woman, Laura, an elegant lady whose energy –as far as I could perceive -was that of a descendant of the *Aztlans*, not a hundred percent from this planet but from other galaxies and frequencies. She had started working for the spiritual awakening years before. She, had a health and beauty clinic where various activities related to the higher self were held. A friend and colleague of hers had organized an event in a hotel. They invited me to participate in the event with a talk about my ancestors and their philosophy.

That is where I met Anabel, the woman that would give me her support throughout my mission in Mazatlan, and throughout the whole awakening project. This person has a huge heart and tremendous energy and has been at my side in all circumstances from the beginning. She's a very evolved spirit. Later on, after meeting new people, I went with this beautiful girl to the clinic where she taught *pilates*. There I continued meeting people who became interested in the Maya philosophy for personal growth.

A few weeks after having met Laura, she invited me to a lecture on quantum physics. After the lecture, a group of people, including me, got together to exchange opinions about the various topics covered in the lecture. Some people asked my opinion, so we talked over coffee and exchanged our views. Among the people with whom I talked was a lady with a beautiful heart, that invited me to an energy vortex near Mazatlan city, in Concordia district. I said "yes" and agreed to meet with her the next week, to walk up the hill called *La Petaca*.

When the day to climb *La Petaca* arrived, we met at my friend's clinic to join other people who were coming with us. The trip to the hill was very happy and pleasant. The group's energy was very good. In *La Petaca* we stayed in a resort cabin whose owner was Armando Nava, a famous local painter. There was light but constant rain. Late at night, we made a ceremony that would reveal to me what we were to do in Mazatlan. After the ceremony, we agreed to climb the hill early the next morning. We had a tranquil and pleasantly chilly night. We got up and had a delicious breakfast, then headed to the top of *La Petaca* hill.

The way up was slow and we could appreciate the indescribably beautiful landscape around us, so full of energetic vibration. When we reached the top, we took a rest and admired the view. Once recovered from the hike, we walked to a rock that had a peculiar shape like a radar dish. Several members of the group held hands next to the stone. While we were meditating in that place, I felt like someone was pulling my body and throwing it from the top of the hill. This did not last long but enough for me to receive plenty of information. It seemed like coded information that would later have to be deciphered. The decoding took place as we hiked down the hill.

Part of the information was that I would have three guides to do the energetic cleansing of the Mazatlan atmosphere. One of them was from *Mexica* descent, and the other two were from *Aztlan* descent. I soon realized these three people were included in the group that went up the hill with me.

We arrived in the resort house at the foot of the mountain and after resting a while and eating, I asked these three people to come with me because I wanted to have a word with them. We went to the side of the house to a group of majestic pine trees. The weather was very pleasant: misty but not cold. I gave them the message I had received as to what I was to do in Mazatlan, and they gladly agreed to help me. I then invited them to meditate with me to promote a closer relationship with one another. While we meditated, a cloud cast a shadow on the hill endowing our meditation with a mystical touch. When we finished and went back to the house, I unexpectedly met one of the first individuals that would follow me in the awakening of the Mexican people: the painter Juan Carlos Valdivia, with whom a profound friendship was established, and with his gracious and beautiful girlfriend as well.

After this interesting and revealing trip, I devoted the next eleven months to giving talks about consciousness, how to liberate low frequency energies trapped in our body, through dance and meditation; I also taught workshops and did ceremonies in different places in Mazatlan, in which different indigenous groups occasionally participated.

It was during these lectures and workshops that I met the future

The Night of the Last Katún 2012 Maya

members of a group with whom I would create a new spiritual frequency. After eleven months of traveling, doing ceremonies and organizing events, the three spiritual guides that were helping me to cleanse Mazatlan's energy, left and went back to their regular activities. However, more people came who were prepared to enter the new energetic frequency that had been generated.

By that time, I had gathered a large group of people that were willing to form a community where free consciousness, meditation and dance would be practiced. So in 2007, we rented a house with a large back yard in a rather run-down condition. But the unity and good will of the people in the community transformed it into a livable place. The first activity we organized there was a relay 120 hour meditation. It was a very satisfying experience to see the unity and enthusiasm of the people.

During the purification of our new center I had an encounter with my ancestors, who revealed to me that a change of consciousness would begin in this place and, therefore, the vibration frequency of that house would rise. When I heard this I could already imagine the results. Most members and visitors started to run away, in other words, they abandoned the community. It puzzled me greatly, but the community's Mayan name gives a rather eloquent answer to the puzzle: *Oxlahum* means thirteen awakened people.

After a few months, approaching 2008, I asked during a meditation, why thirteen and not eleven or twelve? Why not fifteen or twenty? My ancestors' answer was: "If humans were totally awake, the effort of one person only would suffice to generate a new consciousness, but because low frequency thoughts dwell in people's minds, thirteen individuals are needed form the first high frequency spiritual molecule". So I decided to initiate a program based on the integration of various aspects of life to generate the new consciousness that will awaken our country spiritually. And that is how I began to form this new group.

As months went by, I picked the garden as my working place so I would be connected to the Earth to heal it. Here I worked together with the people that were still in the community. The number of members would vary between nine and fourteen.

I was a bit worried because I didn't have enough energy to create the new molecule; I could not gather the necessary *Oxlahum* energy (thirteen people); because they weren't committed enough to work for a common cause nor free of low energies (negative emotions). However, the few people that remained in the community worked very hard.

A few days later, Manolo and Alicia arrived in a very peculiar way. They were looking for a shaman to marry them by the indigenous ritual. They came to me because they had seen me in an interview on the local television station.. They are a charming couple.

Half way through the year, I realized I still didn't have enough people to initiate my mission.. However, my wish was so strong that, under my own risk, I decided to continue. In order to take the next step, the presence of a representative of each of the main cultures (a Mexica and an Aztlán) was required. I needed them to initiate a great movement. Time revealed to me who they were, and whom I could count on completely to begin my mission.

2. U xuul ta´ an
(The last message)

A week before the lunar eclipse of August 16, 2008, I gathered the members of the *Oxlahum* group for a meeting (Anabel, Mike, Rebeca, Rosa Delia, Efraín, J. Carlos, Lili, Marce, Isela, Isabel, Humberto, Lupita, Mary, Ismael, Alicia and Manolo). I informed them about the historical moment we were going through and about the importance of this natural event. I also informed them that a certain number of people were required to do the ceremony on the special day of the eclipse. I asked all of them to participate in the creation of a symbol that would represent unity, the beginning of the Universe and the number thirteen. This number represented, for the Maya, the ultrasound, the highest spiritual vibration connecting us to the super consciousness.

The following days, several members turned in their suggestions. They included things like: the symbol of infinity, spirals, beams and other ideas that came to our minds. One day something special came up, and because we were all on the same frequency, we were able to access higher energetic levels. Efrain had a spiritual experience that I herein relate as it was told:

"The dawn of August 11th, 2008, I dreamed that I was sitting on the beach, facing the ocean; it was a beautiful sunset. Suddenly, someone came to me; it was an elder, an old man. He sat next to me and we started talking about several topics: the sunset, the sea, life, etc. Among other things, he told me: "I'm going to show you a very simple drawing where you can appreciate the symbol of the infinite; one of the most used outlines in ancient civilizations, like the all-seeing eye and the great mind of *Hunab Ku*.. He took a stick approximately 60 cm. Long (2 ft.); put it in my hands and with his hand he guided mine to draw the outline on the wet sand. When it was finished, he took his leave saying: 'If you stare at this drawing carefully for a few minutes, you will see more than the direct eye can see.

"When I woke up the next morning, I couldn't stop thinking about that dream. When I arrived at my office, I took a pencil and reproduced the drawing from my dream. After observing it carefully for a few minutes, I could see the silhouette of a man meditating in the lotus position, seen from above. I've always thought that the best meditation is the one you do with yourself. We are so carried away by our daily life, talking with people, making phone calls, immersed in the computer, chatting on line, etc., that we don't realize how much of our life time is spent on that activity. How different life would be if only we could tap directly our limitless inner source of energy. That is what the symbol represents to me. I wish every person that sees it, uses it or wears it will feel the connection with their inner God and will contact Him, never becoming separate again."

That same evening, Efrain visited the community to share with me his spiritual experience and, together with the other group members , mainly Mike (who is very good at technical art and publicity), we completed the symbol representing unity, harmony and balance of all the things we have around us. We added some beams representing the sun, then some triangles at the sides, joined through a curved line, symbolizing the physical-spiritual duality, like the two serpents in the Aztec calendar. Then, we added two parallel lines below representing water. At the same time, the two bottom lines and the three circles of the design also represent *Oxlahum*, that is, the number thirteen but in a rather artistic form.

Finally, in the center we placed *Hunab Ku's* image symbolizing the coming of the new energy to Earth, forecasted by the two astronomical events of the last *katún* (last twenty years of the Mayan no-time): the 1999 sun eclipse, clearly visible in our country, and the lunar eclipse on August 16th, 2008.

The Night of the Last Katún 2012 Maya

We cleansed the atmosphere with a ceremony that marked the beginning of the new mental frequency (of unity, sharing and peace) on the night of the lunar eclipse. We gathered a good thirty people for the occasion, and for the first time, we shared the symbol with them and explained its meaning.

When I was explaining the symbol, a brief contact was produced with my ancestors. It happened so quickly I could only grasp the following message: The symbol we had created had a much deeper and personal meaning for me. I had a spiritual insight that revealed that the symbol represented a person in meditation. That person was actually me! They told me I had to organize a thirteen day continuous meditation, outdoors, facing the sea, in the sunlight (again the sunlight was an aid for activating the spiritual connection).

That's how the meditation had to be done. By then, I already knew where we could do the meditation as part of the preparation to initiate my mission. The place was exactly the same plaza where I had sat when

The Night of the Last Katún 2012 Maya

I first arrived in Mazatlan, and where I thought about the work that lay ahead. It was the same plaza where I had done several meditations during the last two years. And it was a place where high frequency sounds could be transmitted through the flattened top of the mountain facing the plaza (when you have the chance to visit this place, stand near the arcade where the diving act takes place; clap and you'll hear a peculiar sound). This is the Sánchez Taboada square, also known as El Clavadista (the diver).

3. U su' utia' al Maya' ob
(The return of the Maa' Yab people)

March 21st, day of the spring equinox, is one of the days Maya fans as well as tourists and nature lovers await with great enthusiasm. Early in the morning people gather on one of the flanks of the main pyramid known as the *Chichen Itzá* castle, eager to see the famous light and shadow phenomenon of the sun. As time goes by, more people from different states and also from abroad gather in that place. There are *dancers* doing their ceremonies. People of different creeds, ages, languages, social class, cultures gather together with one purpose: contemplating the thousands of years old phenomenon: the return of *Kukulk'an Quetzalcoatl:* the plumed serpent.

Precisely at noon, the intense sun beams pour down over the pyramid, an ancient building perfectly aligned, astronomically.Then *Kukulk'an Quetzalcoatl* appears. The first beams hit the upper edge of the pyramid and, as the sun follows its cosmic course, it produces the shadow effect on the different levels of the pyramid, colliding against a central wall flanking the main staircase. The shadow resembles a serpent crawling all the way down the staircase, where lies a huge stone serpent head. Definitely, *Kukulk'an Quetzalcoatl* -the plumed serpent- will continue to astonish the world.

I wish to draw your attention to a certain aspect here: *Kukulk'an Quetzalcoatl* can bring people of different walks together, regardless of race, religion, creed, sex or age; it's capable of bringing everyone together.

Our ancestors left us this legacy to demonstrate that just as all of these different people can get together to see this spectacle, all human beings can also live together in harmony and unity. *Kukulk'an Quetzalcoatl* is not a myth; it is a high frequency spiritual state of awareness capable of bringing to you, and to the whole world, understanding about what we are doing on planet Earth.

Sut' u suutukoob! (The moment to awaken the Plumed Serpent has arrived!) It is the moment for you to activate your genetic code as a child of the new sun, as the child of loving light, harmony and balance that you are.

We can all enter such a state of awareness if we stop competing and, instead, learn to live together and share our spirituality, no matter what our beliefs. The moment anticipated and prophesied by our ancestors has arrived! They have high hopes you will understand their messages of light for us to promote a new consciousness of peace, abundance, prosperity, harmony and synchrony with the Universe. I am certain that if you assume your responsibility in this and join the awakening of consciousness, we will make the vision of the *Maa Yab* elders come true by 2012.

From August 30 to September 12 of the year 2008, I prepared myself through a thirteen day continuous meditation, 24 hours a day, on the Sánchez Taboada square in Mazatlan. I sat there on a chair with a poster next to me that said:

> "I WANT A UNITED AND PEACEFUL MEXICO, AND I'M
> WILLING TO DO SOMETHING EVERY DAY UNTIL I
> ACCOMPLISH THIS… WHAT ABOUT YOU? (13 DAY
> MEDITATION)"

For thirteen days, I had the chance to meet different people that offered a variety of comments. I heard them say that peace would never be reached, that only God could do it and He didn't need our help. There were also comments of very high spiritual vibration to the point that some people sat down to meditate with me. People of other religions came and shared their viewpoints with me, with total respect for what I was promoting.

During my meditation period, I met people who were already "awake"; but also people whose ego and religious fanaticism would not let them open to the new era of unity and sharing. The experiences I had during the thirteen days of meditation allowed me to anticipate the situations I was to face and, thus, how I should initiate the awakening of consciousness. During my meditation, my ancestors told me I should begin as a *Ximbal mac tia' al a' hal* (Walker for Peace). As the days went by, we took the first step to unify consciousness. Manolo decided to come with me during the walk for peace. He was a representative of the *Mexicas* and was ready to join my mission. Only a representative of the *Aztlans* was missing; it could well have been Alicia, but she still had a few work commitments to attend to. Some time had to pass, before I knew whether she was going to join the group or not.

On the ninth or tenth day of our meditation in Sanchez Taboada square at 8 pm., a young man came to us. He was slim, with long hair, he wore a shirt and trousers down to the knees and, most noticeably, he was carrying an African-type drum called *jembe*.

We were playing native music when he came; he just stared at us. Then, I asked a member of our group to ask him to play his drum with us to enrich the music, and he immediately said "yes". When the meditation finished and most spectators and companions had left, I was able to converse with this young man. I asked him who he was, what he did, and he told us that he was one of the Taboada divers that entertained the tourists. From that day on, he stayed and kept me company during my meditation, and also in other activities. I realized he had come to us as the third spiritual member, representing the *Aztlan* people that I needed to carry on with my mission. The team was then complete to begin the mission. Meanwhile, Alicia was concluding her work commitments, and would catch up with us later.

This thirteen day physical-spiritual practice was the forerunner of the national movement I'm working on. I intend to unite our country through meditation and cultural sharing as we walk through all the states of the country, with groups and individuals who are willing to put aside their ego and their differences. It will be a movement for unity in our country.

I had to publish this book as soon as possible to bring to light the legacy of my ancestors. I asked Marce -a member of the original group in

The Night of the Last Katún 2012 Maya

Mazatlan- to help me transcribe all the information, which took us many days of intense work.

What we needed was to finish our meditation practice in order to resume the next journey.

Walker for Peace

4. Ximbal mac tia' al a' hal
(Walker for peace)

During the thirteen day meditation outdoors, a fundamental story concerning "our ancestors departure and return" -that my grandparents used to tell me- came to my mind:

When I was approximately eight years old, I remember we were sitting in what we referred to as the kitchen: this was a round construction made of intertwined thin tree trunks that gave the impression of being woven together; the ceiling was made of *huano*, a kind of palm tree that is grown in Yucatan. The house looked somewhat like a pyramid; the kitchen floor was the earth itself, packed down from walking on it over time. Our feet felt the fresh earth because we walked on it barefoot; it was a pleasant sensation. There was a small table in the center where we ate our meals. On one side, my grandmother kept a small fire for the pots where she cooked or lay the grill for the tortillas. It was dinner time; the place was lit by an oil lamp as well as the cooking fire. My grandfather drank his hot chocolate while my sisters Ruby and Tere, and myself, were sitting at the table, with our cups of hot chocolate in front of us, eager to listen to my grandfather's account.

Years ago, in the time of the wise men of the *Maa Yab*, they had established the time of their departure and return, hundreds of years before leaving. In their wisdom, they understood the Earth's cycles. They knew the Earth would go through a stage of deep sleep, so they set up the *Tuunich Quetzal Kíin* (technological stone) in preparation for their departure and return.

They left everything ready in hopes of returning when mother Earth would begin to awaken. To make sure knowledge would not be forgotten and the *nohoch tuunich quetzal kíin* –the *Chichen Itzá* pyramid- would awake in time, the wise elders of each of the main villages (whose energetic transmitters were kept active) gathered with their best men and women.

The Night of the Last Katún 2012 Maya

Among those peoples were the *Aztlans* –the ones that spoke with the ancestors and practiced magic-; the *Mexicas* –the ones who made music and danced-, the *Maa Yab* people –the ones who could see from afar without moving, could talk with the stars and measure time. There were also the ones that integrated knowledge and were great philosophers: the Toltecs.

Night was about to fall and the great ceremonial fire had been prepared. Everyone was sitting around the *Chichen Itzá* pyramid, looking serene, at peace, full of wisdom. There were elders and youth, men and women, all dressed for the occasion. This was the first of the many ceremonial gatherings that would follow.

Far away to the west *baakab* (directon*)*, where the sun sets, you could see the sun a few centimeters off the ground, about to disappear to give way to the moon. There was going to be a full moon that night. All the group members stood up facing the sun, then rested their left knee on the ground, to bring their heart beats closer to Mother Earth. The right knee bent upward, on a 90° angle, their foot firm on the ground, over the Earth. The elders held their beautifully ornamented *Xo'olte ti'i whol* (energetic staff), in their right hand. They stretched their left arm out towards the sun, as though trying to feel its last energetic beams. The rest of the people were in the same position, except both their arms were stretched out towards the sun.

A couple representing each one of the four lineages was sitting in the center of each of the pyramid's four staircases, which faced each *baakab* (cardinal directions). On the North (*xaaman*) were those who talk with their ancestors (Aztlans); on the South (*nohol*) were those who integrated knowledge and shared it with other peoples (Toltects); on the West (*chik iin*) were those who made music and danced and stayed awake awaiting the next dawning (Mexicas). And on the East (*lak iin*) were the men who came from afar, spoke with the stars and measured time, awaiting the arrival of the New Sun (Maa yab).

The women of each of the couples that were in the center were holding a

The Night of the Last Katún 2012 Maya

torch made of tree resin. The men held their *Bajun huubo' ob (conches)* When the last sun beam hid on the horizon, the men started to blow their conches in harmony, and women immediately brought their torches closer to light the ceremonial fire, which illuminated the pyramid. The *Bajun tu' unkulo' ob (ceremonial* drums made of tree trunks, similar to those of the Mexicas) started to vibrate. The *Macobo' ob ka' ak* (men who are synchronized and harmonized with fire) immediately walked towards the ceremonial pyre to light their torches and place them along the pyramid's staircases, bestowing a mystical and energetic touch, attuned with the moment. The great gathering had begun.

The meeting lasted several suns with their moons (130 hours of today). Each elder spoke about what would have to be done in order to preserve the knowledge while the Earth slept and, most of all, they told the gathering which of the peoples were to become the guardians of the power conch, to control and guide other peoples, as they awaited their return.

The representative of each people set forth his knowledge and wisdom. After each of them shared their knowledge and experiences, they made some agreements, which the elders would convey to their people upon their return. Each wise elder climbed to the top of the pyramid at the last part of the ceremony.

The people who integrated knowledge (*The Toltecs*) who had been spokesmen at the last meeting, said:

"We, the elders have reached an agreement for our departure and return. Due to its characteristics, the conch is to represent our peoples who live a harmonious, free and progressive life. Its vibrations bring us in touch with Nature, the Cosmos and, most of all, with one another. We are all One and each one is the Totality. The people that talk with the spirits, those who dance waiting for the new dawn, and those who talk with the stars, and we, the Toltecs, have always lived in unity. The Earth is about to fall asleep as are our descendants on Earth. Such an event will prevent them from using our knowledge, thus, our technology will go unseen by them.

The Night of the Last Katún 2012 Maya

"However, we wish to preserve our knowledge, because at the time of the last *katún (the twenty year period beginning with the end of the Mayan calender in 1992),* the great *Tuunich Quetzal Kiin* (pyramid) in each town can become active again."

Then they agreed to divide the conch into three parts (Aztlans, Mexicas, Maa yab; each of the three peoples becoming guardians of each region – according to their respective attributes and talents- (the Toltecs did not participate as a fourth group, however, they helped to direct and organize the forming of the three groups).

They continued;

" At the same time, special lineages will be created to preserve the essence of our knowledge. This knowledge can be interpreted in advance in order to activate the *Tuunich Quetzal Kiin* (pyramid) on our return.

"Only when the three parts of the conch come together and its sound is heard again, will *Kukulk'an Quetzalcoatl* be ready to come back to Earth, to lead the awakening of the children of the New Sun.

"So from now on, each people shall create its own traditions and ceremonies to keep the Knowledge alive. In our pyramids, in our clothing, in our ceremonies, we shall leave the key to the codices, for them to be easily interpreted. Only those who reach unity and are capable of activating the *Tuunich Quetzal Kiin (pyramid)* can guide our people to freedom, harmony, abundance and evolution, towards the New Sun."

It was then that we heard my grandmother's voice, prompting us to finish our chocolate because it was getting cold. My grandfather's style for telling stories was thrilling; it captured our attention completely. After supper, we went out to the patio to watch the stars; he continued his account about the new consciousness, and the keys to activate the *tunich quetzal kín* so our ancestors could come back.

The Night of the Last Katún 2012 Maya

When the thirteen day meditation concluded on September 20th, 2008, the tremendous task we had in our hands began: a great mission, a *nohoch meyah* (great task) as we would say in Maya. The task was to awaken the Mexican people, to wake up the plumed serpent inside each individual; to make people aware that peace must be practiced daily. Also, the sites where the *Tunich Quetzal Kin* had to be activated had to be found. It was in this spirit that we started a walk throughout the whole country. We committed ourselves to walking every day until we could reach this objective and also to find the people who are aware that the moment has arrived to create a new thought frequency, and are willing to change in order to create a better world.

We named ourselves "Walkers for peace". We are walking the country, giving people our ancestors' messages of light, so that they raise their vibration frequency and start generating ultrasonic frequencies for the awakening of our country, as preparation for the year 2012.

I initiated the walking journey in the North, with Alicia and Manolo. He became the Hayoka of the group through Tata Cachora, a Yaqui Indian who lives in Cerro Azul, Baja California state. A Hayoka is one who tries to detour you from your path so that you remain constantly aware of your mission.

Alicia became the healer of the group. She is from *Aztlan* descent; her hands have healing power and are able to move energy. As a woman, she represents the energetic balance and the frequencies that we are awakening throughout the country.

We visited indigenous, religious, cultural and philosophical leaders -and others- motivating them to seek unity. We participated with them in ceremonies, meditation sessions and events where each group contributed their own traditions and beliefs, and we gave them our messages of light. We had lots of experiences during that time: people helped us, they received us in their homes. On occasions, we even slept in the desert, in gasoline stations, in the street, in town gazebos. We endured hunger, extreme heat, cold, rain, all kinds of experiences.

The Night of the Last Katún 2012 Maya

Motivated by the idea of awakening the people, different kinds of individuals joined us and helped us in our activities. Eighteen people of different religions and ethnic groups were with me. Walking and being together twenty four hours a day exhausted them. They were not quite prepared to carry out such a task in a continuous fashion, so one by one they gave up. Nevertheless, their support meant a lot to us and was important at that moment; they cared for us, protected us and encouraged us to continue on with our mission.

When we arrived in Guadalajara, Jalisco state, the last walkers left us, but then others came. The people that walk with us come and go, sometimes there's a lot of us, some times just a few. Hayoka, Alicia and myself remain together as the group's core in pursuit of our goal.

We carried on our mission until we arrived at the port of Manzanillo, Colima state, in July 2009. When we arrived there, I immediately felt the good energy of the city. I told the group something very relevant to the awakening of consciousness was to going take place, and that we had to open a portal of light there to create the first vibration frequency to awaken the people. All we had was a sincere heart and much enthusiasm to fulfill our mission. We then tried to contact leaders that people referred us to, but with no success because we had arrived in the place without previous notice; perhaps also because they were busy people and couldn't come. So, not knowing anybody and with no more contacts to make, once again, we slept downtown. Fortunately, the weather was good.

The next day, the guys walked around in search of people or groups who might be interested in hearing our message; that's how we found the Sai Baba people who offered us lodging on a patio where they taught yoga, and that's where we gave our first talks in the port of Manzanillo. Right from the first talk, we met people who showed willingness to help us in our mission. They joined us as external members because most of them had steady jobs in the communication media.

The day after transmitting the messages of light, John Polo, Ezael, Alex,

The Night of the Last Katún 2012 Maya

Aida, Antonio, Javier and Ruben offered selfless help to provide me whatever I needed to carry out my mission. Later, Adriana, Alonso and Luis and other people joined us in the project. We were very pleased to find out that there are people who are really willing to do something to improve things and open up the path for our country to reach a higher spiritual frequency. In that meeting, I mentioned to them that we needed to open a portal of light to transmit ultrasonic frequencies, for which we needed two things: finding the right place and building a pyramid as an energetic generator. Everyone had to think what the ideal site for that purpose could be.

We looked around for one week, visiting the beaches, mountains and we joined the *temazcaleros* [those who lead the *temazcal*: a sweat lodge] to become acquainted with them. That is how many people ended up joining us in the project, until one of them took us to a place in the mountains, just outside of town. This had been an archeological site that was now destroyed and covered by the earth. But, lo and behold, the owner of this beautiful place had built a "dome" there. The structure, design and orientation of the building involved ancient technology. He had this construction made of clay, with hand-made wall finishing; the dome was aligned with the four cardinal directions. The upper wall or ceiling formed the "Quetzalcoatl cross". The whole building was mathematically and astronomically aligned with the planet Venus (*L'amat* in Mayan language). And Venus is the keystone in Maya philosophy as the base of their astronomical knowledge and calendar. I jumped with joy. Can you imagine how I felt when I discovered this? What is a building with the same functions of a pyramid doing in the middle of a mountain range surrounded by vegetation?

Coincidence? Certainly not! There are awakened people who know their planetary mission today. This was the case of the person who built this "dome", which is nothing less than a vibration machine like the ones our ancestors had. It's a modern *Tunich Quetzal Kin* (technological stone or pyramid).

What we needed now was to meet the owner to get his permission to use the site for free, because we had no money to rent it. We trusted he would hear our plea and agree to help us in this important step that would activate the first ultrasonic frequency.

A few days went by before Ezael called me to tell me he had arranged a meeting with the owner. The day of the appointment, we went with Ezael and some of the walkers to the agreed place. John Polo caught up with us there. We had the interview with Hugo Herrera, who happened to be a very agreeable and knowledgeable person. He participated in a circle of fire from the Mexica tradition. We shared our mutual experiences, and I forwarded him the project plan I had in mind. After listening to me and analyzing the project he gave us an affirmative answer, and told us he was willing to help us with the event. The news made us very happy and grateful to this good hearted man.

Then we buckled down to planning a strategy to activate the portal of light. We had the place, now we needed to devise a way to activate the energy; the same one I had received during a meditation. Thirteen spiritual and/or indigenous leaders were required: to eliminate the resentment and pain frequency caused by the conquest, and second, to achieve the unity of creeds and philosophies so they could live next to each other peacefully.

We immediately conceived a plan: inviting thirteen leaders out of those we had met during our walk in the North of the country. There was one inconvenience though: we would have to pay their transportation, meals and lodging and those of their escorts as well. Some were coming in groups of four to ten people. We didn't have the money for all of them, so we had to plan a different strategy. With the help of our supporters, we looked for potential sponsors. I invited friends and groups we had met during our walk throughout the country and suggested people pay a donation to participate in the event, to finance the expenses of the invited leaders.

On October 4th, 2009, the first part of the vision I had in the *Cholula* pyramid in Puebla, came true. I invited the thirteen leaders to meditate for one hundred and thirty continuous hours in the dome. They all came on time. There were *Yaqui* and *Kumiai* tatas (wise elders) and leaders, members of the *Mexica* circles of fire, *Yoreme* and *Wirrarika* shamans, the guardians of the Colima volcanoes, Sai Baba devotes, the Warriors of Light, Transcendental Meditation Masters (of the Maharishi line) , the *Pneuma* group, the Dance of the Heart group, the *Zapaliname* group. All of them made their ceremonies during the 130 hour meditation, in unity, harmony and togetherness. At the end of the meditation on October 4th, at 1:12 am, the full moon appeared through the opening at the top of the dome.. At 1:13 pm the largest ceremony for the unity of all peoples began, to create the vibration frequency that would bring the annihilation of the negativity in our country one step forward. It lasted forty minutes, from the moment the full moon appeared it was cheered with dances, chants, meditation, vibrations, that continued until the end of the ceremony. Everyone was focused on one objective: raising the consciousness of the country.

We' have taken the first step: the portal of light has been opened. We are still walking throughout the country preparing new events to wake up our brothers and sisters. The walk will continue until the next portals, one in El Tajín, Veracruz state –which will be a continental event- and then the grand gathering in Chichen Itzá, Yucatan state –that will involve the whole world.

You can be part of the awakening of the children of the New Sun.

5. Ka´anal Humm
(How to create the frequency of unity, harmony and consciousness)

Why is it that although groups and individuals want peace in our country, everything remains the same or even looks worse than ever? I will answer the question with a metaphor.

Imagine you are standing in front of a slope; there is a large rock next to you that you wish to take all the way to the top, and you have ten friends that are willing to help, but not all of them can help you at the same time. One of them offers to help at ten in the morning, another one says he can help at three in the afternoon, still another person tells you he cannot help before eight in the evening.

Do you think you'd be able to move the rock? Obviously not, your efforts and the staggered efforts of your friends would be useless. The same thing is happening with all of those people who want peace.

There are many religions, philosophies and movements for peace, and there are many people who yearn for a style of life different from the one they have. Unfortunately, people can help at different moments as in the case of the rock. But what would happen if your ten friends got together and could all push the rock at the same time? It's clear they could move the rock and place it where you wanted it. Exactly the same thing happens with people's consciousness.

If we could all get together on the same days, at the same time, simultaneously send our prayer, meditation, positive thinking to the Universe (each according to his religion and creed), we could gather enough energy to create a new frequency and have peace become a habit. That's why I'm proposing the following:

Help us create the frequency for unity, peace and harmony. Every day at 12 pm (noon in the center of the country) and at 10 pm, do any of the following for 21 minutes:

The Night of the Last Katún 2012 Maya

- Take some time off and pray, meditate for peace, unity and the awakening of the consciousness, according to your own beliefs.

- You can also visualize the meditation of the First Message of Light: the "potter" meditation. (See page 62)

- As a last suggestion, take a fine glass cup with water, wet your fingers and rub the rim of the cup with a circular movement, producing a vibration (sound). Pray or meditate for 20 or 30 minutes, as you continue to rub the rim of the cup.

Do this every day to eliminate resentment, pain and suffering of the Mexican people. Slowly, we will replace the negative thinking with the new peace, unity and harmony frequency. Let's do it together until we get results. If you're still at work or in school at that time, or driving your car, or you simply don't have a crystal cup at hand, you can pray or, if you prefer, you may repeat the following Mayan mantra: *Sucum Yumm cu cuxtal in tech yetel ten*, which means: "Brother, God abides in you and in me."

You're probably wondering why use the cup? The frequency produced by glass cups, or any objects that let off acute but soft sounds, accelerates the neuron movement and, like the pyramids, transmits the energy of your intention or that of your prayer, meditation, or positive thinking to everything around you. The energy of intention is so strong it can modify the behavior of others. Cups are important in as much as they can transmit messages as pyramids do; also because they generate the kind of frequencies required by the messages of light -high vibration spiritual messages- to come through:. They cannot transmit negative messages or low frequency vibrations.

Another reason why I suggest using a cup or objects producing acute sounds is because you can create curiosity in the people around you and, thus, motivate them to do the same thing. The most important thing here is that the sound and the intention will begin to create unity and togetherness, regardless of people's beliefs. Only working together to create peace is important.

So it doesn't matter where you are at that moment. If you wish something strongly enough, I'm sure you will help other people become involved, just by praying, meditating and/or producing the sound vibration on your cup. Recommend this book to your friends, relatives, neighbors; explain our purpose to them.

I wish to clarify: we are not looking for followers, nor promoting a certain philosophy; we are uniting and motivating people so we can live as one body, in peace and harmony!

Listen, please, the time for fear is over, we have no more time for ignorance, this is a time for mutual understanding. Think about it, and realize that what I'm telling you is an elevated truth.

6. U xuul katún
(The time of no-time)

Another one of the messages that the Maya left us is about the "time of no-time". It is about the nights of the last *katún* that we are living through, it's a period of darkness (metaphorically speaking) and lack of responsibility in humans. The time of no-time is the prior step to collective consciousness, to the consciousness of unity and of **PEACE IN MEXICO** and in all **THE WORLD**.

We are living through the best period in the history of humanity, and you are participating in it. There is no reason for us not to be able to achieve unity and peace. I know you might be very busy working, you may not have time, but this is a crucial and historical moment for humanity. You must make a double or triple effort to make time to be part of it and create the habit of peace.

Many people probably think this is nonsense and hold on to their traditional hasty and agitated lifestyle, and probably think this unity thing does not concern them. But if we don't reach unity in our country, things are going to become more difficult, and everything you've treasured and fought for –like the family, work, money, material goods-, might be lost in just the blink of an eye.

It is the moment to get down to doing something for ourselves: first, for our inner peace, and then, for peace around us.

Beware because you may come across leaders with big egos and little spirituality. When you get to know them, you see whether their guidance is capable of bringing people together, or whether you will have to do it by yourself.

7. Paakat a chiikul
(Observe the signs)

Watch the signs around you; you can't close your eyes to what's happening on our planet and on humans' consciousness. I'll give you some recent examples:

The Olympic Games.- The host country of the Olympic Games in August 2008 was the city of Beijing, China. The Chinese culture was closed to the world for a long time. The Olympic Games were an example of the country's opening up to the world, and it was a clear example of the expansion of the world's consciousness and its preparation for a moment we didn't think would arrive.

On the other hand, the headquarters of the next Olympic Games of 2012 will be London, a European city, under the slogan of cultural opening where all cultures and philosophies must be accepted and respected; which is no different from the philosophy of *Kukulk´an Quetzalcoaltl's* return.

 Global Warming- What's happening to the planet? The Earth is getting ready to activate the remaining DNA codes through heat, but your participation with high frequency spiritual thoughts is needed. The world has split in two: those who hurt the Earth, and those who try to save the planet. And you: what side are you on? Which of the two sides will prevail?

Science, especially Quantum Physics.- Modern life and the technological progress of the world have been sending clues or messages telling us that we are energy, that our thoughts affect our actions. Quantum Physics tells us that we can create everything we can imagine; we can modify matter by just observing it; that we are the masters of our thinking; that we can create our own life. So, what are you waiting for?

The Night of the Last Katún 2012 Maya

Eclipses and the Maya legacy.- The astronomical events, such as sun and moon eclipses prophesied by the Maya for the last *katún* as a sign of the awakening, have been mathematically exact.

The Maya: "Marvel of the World".- The fact that the Mayan culture became known to the whole world is not a coincidence, nor the fact that the *Chichen Itzá* castle was elected as one of the world's seven marvels. Apart from the architectural beauty of this monument, the construction is full of symbolism, and it congregates tens of thousands of people of different races, creeds, religions, cultures, age and social class around it. Every year, people gather in *Chichen Itzá* to watch the light and shadow phenomenon of the plumed serpent. What other signs do you need to become convinced that your participation and responsibility in the awakening process is needed? Aren't you tired of the world as it is today?

All that you need is to accept yourself as God and as part of It at the same time. In other words, you are the whole and a molecule of the whole, simultaneously. Don't stay behind; whatever your philosophy is join us in the awakening. Get others involved and talk with them about the creation of a new mental frequency, where the consciousness of love, truth, balance, harmony and peace shall be the leading forces of the world.

Join us and start creating the new frequency through any of the suggested methods, and if you have another positive collective intention practice, send it to our web page.

Let us do something amazing as one united people!

Let's create the habit! Don't do it just one time; do it every day until you've built the habit of thinking only in positive terms.

While you produce the sound on your cup, send positive thoughts to the Universe.

I am sorry to tell you that the awakening cannot be achieved with **ONE** protest act or **ONE** march, **ONE** blackout, or celebrating **ONE** day without smoking, or **ONE** day celebrating the family or the environment. In short, nothing can be achieved with **ONE** massive event. These one-day events are just celebrations to press the government into doing something. But if we think that is the only thing that must be done, we are wrong!

Why don't we celebrate world food day and eat only that day, for that matter? Things don't work out that way, do they? The intention of such one-day events is good, but the consciousness awakening starts when **A HABIT IS BUILT**, when you repeat something enough times to create a mental frequency. It's like when you decide to do exercise. Getting up early the first day won't negate the importance of the remaining three hundred and sixty four days, in the achievement of your goal. When you wish to raise your self-esteem, one day of thinking positive is not enough to change your life; you must do it constantly; the more you do it, the better.

There are many awakened people today. I even think that most people today are aware that they must do something, but although they're aware that they have to do something, they are not willing to go beyond their comfort zone. They are hooked by their hectic life rhythm; they're waiting for others to do it. But if we don't assume our share of the responsibility in the current state of things, and we're just waiting to see what happens, nothing is going to happen!

That is why I'm trying to motivate people to get together every day to create a new vibration and, also, to build the habit of unity, together. If we are united –whether we think differently or not- we can achieve more and reach far.

I repeat, we must be constantly united until we build a habit. Don't let the balance tilt in the wrong direction. We, who want the awakening of consciousness, are more numerous than those who hurt the planet. Now, how many people really yearn for this objective? You will only know when you see who's assuming responsibility and who isn't, who is daring to go beyond their fears, grief, shame, or being afraid of what

The Night of the Last Katún 2012 Maya

others might say. Those who assume responsibility are the ones that will make a difference, and they will make it worthwhile for all humanity to have participated in this world.

There are still a lot of things I wish to tell you, but this book must be published now to help people wake up.

If you have a question or wish to contribute to our Walk for Peace movement, or else you wish to join us, visit our web page.

When I finished writing this book, I received one more message concerning the new frequency and the codices that our ancestors left us that would help us align our energy for the awakening.

If you wish to support the frequency change and the new awakening, I invite you to:

- Forward our e-mail about unity and conscious awakening to others. If you don't have it you can download it from our web page.

- Get one of those bracelets or pendants that generate ultrasonic frequencies. You can be sure that your investment will help people wake up for the change of consciousness.

- Register on our web page and receive our bulletins on events, ceremonies and activities for "The Children of the New Sun"

We are searching for people in each city and country who can help us give talks, lectures and seminars, and who want to join the movement for the 2012 awakening, transmitting "ultrasonic vibrations" to activate energy of a highly spiritual vibration.

The Night of the Last Katún 2012 Maya

Visit us at: www.actah2012.com

Web page: www.elcaminantemaya2012.com Spanish

****

******

**

Glossary

U´ ta' an maya' abo' o (Maya vocabulary)

Ahal - Awakening
Ahau – Lord
Antal - Being
Baakab -Direction
Beet – To do
Cabal Humm – Subsonic
Ch´iha´an- Elder
Éemel – Descending or downward
Ek Balam – Jaguar star
Hets´ - To sooth
Hunab Ku- God
Ka´anal Humm – Ultrasound
K´iinil – Time
Kukulk' an- Plumed Serpent
Maa yab- The not many, the elected
L'amat- Planet Venus
Meyah – Works
Nohoch - Large
Ox - Three
Paachil – Behind
Péek – Movement
P´iis – Measure, moderate
Pixan – Spirit
Suut – Return
Sut' u suutukoob – The moment has arrived
T´aan – Word
 Xíimbal – To walk
Xtub – The last
Xuul – The end

Nahuatl vocabulary

Hue huetl – Ceremonial drum used by the *danzantes* [dancers]
Iztaccihuatl – White woman (sleeping woman), volcano in Puelba state
Popocatepetl – Fuming mountain: volcano in Puebla state
Quetzalcoatl – Plumed serpent